WAHIDA CLARK PRESENTS

THE OFFICIAL SNEAK PEEK

This is a work of fiction. Names, characters, places, and incidents either are the product of the author's imagination or are used fictitiously, and any resemblance to actual persons, living or dead, business establishments, events, or locales are entirely coincidental.

Wahida Clark Presents Publishing
60 Evergreen Place
Suite 904A
East Orange, New Jersey 07018
1(866)-910-6920
www.wclarkpublishing.com

Copyright 2019 © by Wahida Clark Presents
All rights reserved. This book, or parts thereof, may not be reproduced in any form without permission.

Library of Congress Cataloging-In-Publication Data: WCP Sneak Peek 2019
ISBN 13-digit 9781947732698 (paperback)
ISBN 13-digit 9781947732681 (ebook)

LCCN: 201000000
1. Sex - 2. Lies - 3. Infidelity - 4. African American- HIV
5. Homosexuality - 6. Violence - 7.Relationships

Cover design and layout by Nuance Art, LLC
Book design by NuanceArt@wclarkpublishing.com
Edited by Linda Wilson
Proofreader Rosalind Hamilton
Printed in USA

WAHIDA CLARK PRESENTS

Baltimore Raw

A Novel By
AISHA HALL

This is a work of fiction. Names, characters, places, and incidents either are the product of the author's imagination or are used fictitiously, and any resemblance to actual persons, living or dead, business establishments, events, or locales are entirely coincidental.

Wahida Clark Presents Publishing
60 Evergreen Place
Suite 904A
East Orange, New Jersey 07018
1(866)-910-6920
www.wclarkpublishing.com

Copyright 2019 © by Aisha Hall

All rights reserved. This book, or parts thereof, may not be reproduced in any form without permission.

Library of Congress Cataloging-In-Publication Data:
Aisha Hall
Baltimore Raw
    ISBN 13-digit 9781944992590 (paper)
    ISBN 13-digit 9781944992651 (ebook)
    ISBN 13-digit 9781944992637 (Hardcover)

LCCN: 201000000
1. Sex - 2. Lies - 3. Infidelity - 4. African American- HIV –
5. Homosexuality - 6. Violence - 7. Relationships

Cover design and layout by Nuance Art, LLC
Book design by NuanceArt@wclarkpublishing.com
Edited by Linda Wilson
Proofreader Rosalind Hamilton
Printed in USA

Chapter 1

Von

Her wardrobe and shoe collection were so extensive, it took up an entire bedroom-sized walk-in closet. But all those expensive clothes could not satisfy the pain that clamped itself around her heart. So she decided to downsize. She began cutting up her own shit like a madwoman.

Sobbing, she destroyed things that were at one time her prized possessions. She shook her head over and over again, as black tears ran down her cheeks, making her look almost as grim as she felt. Then she heard footsteps running up the staircase, followed by her bedroom door flying open.

"Von! Where are you, girl?" It was her best friend Paige. Paige had been blowing up Von's phone and did not get an answer. So she rushed over to see what was going on. Opening the closet door, Paige discovered Von sitting on the floor in a pile of cut up clothes.

"Girl, what the hell are you doing? Are you crazy! Is that your Chanel dress over there?" She hadn't taken the time to look at Von's face. She was too shocked by the sight in front of her. Von dropped the scissors and put her head between her trembling brown hands. Her cries stabbed against Paige like a dull knife. She squat down in front of her friend and raised her chin. "Oh God! What's wrong, Von? Talk to me!" she said sitting beside her and immediately hugging her.

Von's normally freshly manicured fingernails were broken and chipped. This was not her style at all. Von was a fly chick. She had thick black hair, cut into a long bob. She always looked pretty and perfect—the opposite of how she looked right now.

"You gotta talk to me, Von. Please tell me what's going on," Paige asked in a concerned tone.

"Oh God!" Von said with more tears and even more sobs.

"It's gonna be okay. Whatever it is. We've been through every possible thing ever since we were little girls. Whatever it is, I promise you, it will be okay." She wiped her best friend's tears. The television was loud, drowning out some of Von's sobs. Neither one of the girls paid attention to the report, which talked about Baltimore's body count already being 10 percent higher than it was last year. Paige got up and muted the television. Then she pulled her friend to her feet, and the two of them walked over to Von's plush bed. They both backed up until their backs were supported by Von's plush brown leather headboard.

Von pushed Paige's hands away from her face and jumped off the bed to her feet.

"It's *not* going to be all right! It's not! I'm too young to die so early. Too young, Paige!" she screamed.

"Von what the hell are you talking about? Is somebody after you?"

"No! It's Rodney's fault! I trusted him. That lying, cheating, no-good bastard! He gave me HIV! I got fucking AIDS! That bitch-ass nigga was running around fucking them damn fiends . . . stankin'-ass freaks! Anybody with a hole!" Von paused and wiped her tears away. That same hand appeared to be dipped in diamonds. She was rockin' a diamond bracelet, a gold Rolex, and a giant rock sitting atop a platinum ring—all gifts from the man who she felt had signed her death certificate.

"Oh my God!" is all that Paige could say. She fought back against her emotions, trying to avoid adding to the river of tears that had accumulated in the room already.

"All this fuckin' time . . . He's been out doing me dirty." She shook her head. "I swear to God, Paige, I wish I never met that piece of shit." Paige put her cream-colored hand on Von's honey-brown arm. The contrast had never been more obvious. Paige was about five-six, and Von was taller, about five-eight, with nothing shy of a model figure.

"Girl, you are not going to die. Stop talking like that. Don't you know about the medicine they have these days? You can live a long and normal life," Paige said squeezing Von in a tight embrace. Von did not hug her back.

"I should give this shit to every no-good Tom, Dick, and Harry in the city." The anger in Von's voice stunned Paige. She knew her friend, and she *never* talked like this. Scared that Von might be serious, Paige looked her in the eyes and pointed her finger in her face.

"Now hold up, boo. You are trippin'. I know that is the anger in you speaking. You don't mean that. That shit is dead wrong. You are hurt and upset. We're going to see the best doctors and make sure you get the best care. We will get through this together."

Von's face dropped. Both of them had seen what AIDS had done to Baltimore. It had the highest rate in the country and the numbers were scary. Having unprotected sex in their city could be a death wish. They'd heard people say it, but to see it so up close and personal was beyond disheartening.

It was devastating.

"I thought about it, Paige. I don't want to go out like this. I always said if I ever found myself in a situation that might end my life, I would rather end it myself."

"Girl, are you crazy? Shut up talking like that. You are *only* 18 years old. You have plenty of life to live."

"No, for real. I think I'll just kill myself. Yeah, that's what I'll do."

"No! What you're gonna do is get off that bed and help me get your stuff back on the hangers and hanging back up in the closet. I gotta save the rest of this expensive shit."

"I don't care about none of that shit. Rodney bought it for me."

"So what? Don't cut up your shit."

"And you know what else, Paige . . . I don't think that muthafucka even *knows* he's sick. He's a walking infector."

"Mm mm mm! Girl! Maybe we should just wait until he comes in here tonight, and shoot him in the dick!" Paige said.

"Good idea!" And then the two of them fell out laughing.

"But seriously, Von, you have been there for me and Marla in a way I can never thank you enough for. My own mother didn't want to accept me and my 16-year-old pregnant self. You have been a great godmother to my daughter. And she's getting ready to have a big fourth birthday party. I need you there. So, if you're gonna kill yourself, do it after the party, bitch." Von started laughing, and the two of them fell out again. Then suddenly, Paige stopped laughing and looked at her friend. "I love you, Von. We are going to get through this. I promise."

"Thank you, friend. Well . . . Really, you are more like my sister."

"Man, Nasty is going to flip out."

Von's eyes widened with fear. "No! He will never know. I am *not* going to tell Nasty. Girl, are you crazy. My brother would lose his mind. I would not put his on him. Promise me you will never tell him."

"I promise, okay, okay. Calm down." "You know how he is," Von said.

"I know. Okay, so where is Rodney's ass now?" Paige asked.

"I don't know."

"Well, he's probably running around with that young 16-year-old girl. Her name's Star."

"Star? What are you talking about?" Paige put her head down. "So that rumor *is* true?"

"Look, Von, he's been creeping with her for a while. And I didn't want to tell you. I didn't wanna be the one to destroy your happiness."

"No, instead, you sat there and allowed that bitch-ass clown to destroy my life," Von spat. The truth struck Paige like a hot iron. The last thing she wanted to do was hurt her friend, and she ended up hurting her anyway. Von had been hurt her entire life. Her parents were Baltimore royalty before there was a hit put out on them when Von was just 9 years old. They were both murdered by cold-blooded killers. But those hitters were never found, and their deaths went unaccounted for. They left behind Von and her brother, Nasty.

"Von, come on. It's not like that, and you know it."

"I know that I got fucked over by him. I know it came from him having sex with a bunch of other women. How do I know that she wasn't the one who gave it to him? And that had I known about them messing around, I might have been able to get out of this relationship."

Paige didn't say anything. But they both knew that even if Von had known, she would not have left Rodney. It was just one of those situations that females find themselves in when they are so strung out over a man that they lose themselves. And that's what happened to Von.

"Just accept it. You're part of the reason why I'm sick now."

"I love you, Von. You know this. And I know you're upset. So I'm going to leave and come back tomorrow."

"Yeah, do that!" she spat with venom dripping from her tongue. Paige stepped out of the house, and Von slammed the door behind her. Paige's body jerked with the slamming of the door. It felt like a smack in the face. As she walked to her car tears fell from her eyes. Her friend's pain was her pain, and Von was right. Maybe if she'd said something, Von may have not gotten sick.

In the house, Von sat on the white velvet couch in her living room and opened up the day's mail. She got a letter from her brother, Nasty. Nasty had taken care of her after their parents got killed. She was 9, and Nasty was 13. They came home from school to find their parents dead. Nasty, being too smart for his own good, ran to the neighbors' house. His best friend Soulja lived across the street. Soulja snuck Nasty and Von in his house and hid them out for days.

Soulja's mother, Tilda, let them stay with her. She was no stranger to the dangers of street life. There was no guarantee that whoever killed their parents might come back to finish off the job. So Soulja's family protected Nasty and Von. And they became siblings in every sense of the word.

Even though Nasty was only 13, he took his job as Von's big brother extremely seriously. So did Soulja.

They were obsessed with protecting her, and they were good at it. One time a boy touched Von's butt, and Soulja and Nasty viciously whipped his ass. He vowed to protect her with his life.

Growing up without parents, Nasty stayed in the streets. He wanted his little sister to have the best of the best. So he started robbing niccas. Nasty and Soulja would do whatever was necessary to keep money in their pockets, and they gained a reputation for being young and ruthless.

Nasty was consumed by anger over his parents and had damn near lost respect for people—period. He seemed to hate anybody who wasn't Von or Soulja. Years later, Nasty and Soulja became notorious drug dealers in Baltimore. The two of them were young teenagers, but they were moving more weight than seasoned, grown-ass men. At the age of 18, Nasty and Soulja had tracked down Nasty and Von's parents' killers in Brazil. The two got passports and made their way to Brazil with a guide. It was Soulja's Brazilian baby mother, Teja, who put them onto what she heard had happened. She was almost 30 when she got pregnant by a teenager. But he was more man than any other men she'd ever met.

While they were gone, Nasty left Von in the care of his man Rodney. Rodney had promised to look out for young Von while they were gone. But Nasty and Soulja had no idea how much of a snake Rodney really was.

When Soulja and Nasty got back from their trip, the feds were waiting for them. They were arrested at the airport. The two of them got stuck in prison, and young Von got stuck with Rodney.

WAHIDA CLARK PRESENTS:

LUST NOW, CRY LATER

A Novel
by
Tahanee

Copyright 2019 © Tahanee

All rights reserved. No part of this publication may be reproduced or distributed in any form or by any means, electronic or mechanical, including photocopying, recording, or by any information storage or retrieval system, without the prior written consent of the author. This is a work of fiction. Names, characters, places, and incidents either are the product of the author's imagination or are used fictitiously, and any resemblance to actual persons, living or dead, business establishments, events, or locales are entirely coincidental.

Wahida Clark Presents Publishing
60 Evergreen Place
Suite 904A
East Orange, New Jersey 07018
1(866)-910-6920
www.wclarkpublishing.com

Copyright 2019 © by Tahanee Sayyid
All rights reserved. This book, or parts thereof, may not be reproduced in any form without permission.

Library of Congress Cataloging-In-Publication Data:
Tahanee
Lust Now Cry Later
ISBN 13-digit 9781947732292 (paper)
ISBN 13-digit 9781947732315 (ebook)
ISBN 13-digit 9781947732308 (Hardcover)
LCCN: 2018906371

1. Sex - 2. Domestic violence - 3. Washington DC - 4. African American- HIV - 5.Homosexuality - 6. Violence - 7. Relationships - 8. New Jersey – 9. Suspends

Cover design and layout by Nuance Art, LLC
Book design by $weet & Tasty Visual Arts
www.artdiggs.com
Edited by Linda Wilson
Proofreader Rosalind Hamilton

July 24, 2002
Prologue

"Well, looks like it's just you and me, kiddo." Sdia's Great Uncle George winked, closing the door behind him. Walking past her, he reached down and pinched her on her buttocks.

Eight-year-old Sdia quickly grabbed her behind and frowned. She let out a yelp. "Ouch!" *That wasn't nice!* she thought.

"Come on over here and let me see how big you've grown." Uncle George chuckled, tickled by her reaction. He placed one hand over his semi-erect penis and reclined in the seat with the other. "I'm waiting," he sang.

Sdia looked down at the faux wood floor, rather confused as to what was going on. She leaned both feet to the side, occasionally bringing them in and out as her dress followed the rhythm, swaying back and forth. Something just didn't feel right. *I wish Mommy could have taken me to work with her, instead of leaving me here with Uncle George. I hope she comes back soon!*

"Come on now," he teased, pulling on a piece of cotton that had seeped from out of the arm of the chair. "Don't tell me you're shy. I saw you over there earlier, dancing to the sound of the wind chimes, or as you say, *dingles*. I know you didn't come all the way to Maryland from DC to stand in a corner." He seductively twirled the cotton around his long triangular-shaped fingernails and smiled.

Sdia's eyes remained glued to the floor as she continued to balance her weight on both ankles.

"I don't bite." He gave a low belly laugh. "Come here." He motioned with his index finger, studying her every movement. Sdia began to fidget with her fingers. *What is going on? Uncle George is looking at me. I'm not going to look up; I don't want to look at him!*

"Those sure are some pretty shoes," he said, referring to the light pink jellies she wore.

She abruptly stopped titling her ankles and looked at her shoes. Her chapped lips slowly parted. "My mommy bought them," she whispered, slowly raising her eyes from the floor until they were greeted by her Uncle George's joker-like smile.

"You're going to mess up those beautiful shoes by tilting your feet like that. You wouldn't want to mess up those shoes, now—would you?"

"No," she mumbled.

"Exactly." George nodded, leaning forward and squinting. "I like your dress. Are those roses?"

Sdia looked down at her dress. "These aren't roses; they're sunflowers." Her voice broke off into a whine.

"No. Those are roses."

"Nuh-uuuhn," she sang, shaking her head no. "Uh-huuhn," he mocked, nodding yes.

Sdia gave him a blank gaze.

"Those are rosy rose roses." Uncle George spoke with his tongue partially exposed, imitating Donald Duck.

Sdia giggled. "Uncle George. These are sunflowers." She pointed to one of the flowers on her dress. "Roses are red."

"Maybe you're right. You know Uncle George can't see that well." He squinted. "Can you come a little closer so that I can get a better look?" His eyes widened.

Bashfully, Sdia looked down.

"Come on. It's okay, sweetie," he promised.

Sdia slowly raised her head, and bit by bit, cautiously walked toward him; the old wooden floors squeaked beneath her feet.

"That's right. Come on and sit right here." He excitedly motioned her to sit on his lap. "Hurry, hurry, hurry," he squealed, fanning both hands wildly as if he'd touched a hot surface. Sdia held out her small hand and placed it into his.

George quickly pulled her down onto his lap, positioning her buttocks on top of his penis. Sdia quickly jumped up and looked down at her uncle's lap. *What was that? What did I just sit on?* "I want Mommy," Sdia blurted out with a frown.

"Your mama's at work. She won't be back till later this evening," he reminded her, pulling her closer, until they were face to face.

"I tell you what? How about you sit in the big red chair?" He smiled, revealing a mouthful of brown teeth.

Sdia scrunched up her nose as the stench of decaying teeth and rotten egg hit her directly in the face. *Uncle George's breath smells like doo-doo.*

He stood, placed both hands under her arms, and lifted her into the chair. The ridged, torn pieces of leather clawed at her arms and legs, leaving unpleasant long white scratches as he scooted her backward. "Woo wee! You sho' is heavy," he grunted, standing straight up and dusting his hands together. Slowly he kneeled down to adjust the seat back until it couldn't go any further. "Comfy?" he asked, taking a step back with his hands in his pocket. Sdia stared down at the flowers on her dress.

"I swear you look just like your mama when she was younger," he said, gazing down at her. "You know she used to love to come and visit me when she was younger. Do you know what her favorite game was?" George squatted beside her as a gust of hot air and the scent of Old Spice rushed her nostrils. "I'll give you a hint. The itsy bitsy spider …" he began to sing, giving her a quick wink. "Came up the water spout …" His warm, wrinkled fingers glided across her thighs …"Down came the rain and washed the spider out."

I want my mommy. I want to go home! Sweat beads formed on Sdia's back and the back of her thighs. She squirmed in the chair as the warm leather latched onto her skin. *I want to get up! I don't like this!* She stretched her neck far back, poked out her chest and clenched the tattered arms of the chair, trying to pull herself up.

"Just relax!" George said, placing his hand on her chest and shoving her back. She fell backward and quickly closed her eyes. *I want my mommy!* Her uncle continued to run his fingers up her thighs, his breathing grew heavier; the hot air from his mouth and nose landed on her knee caps, sending chills up her spine.

She then tried focusing on the wind chimes jingling in the far distance. *The dingles! The dingles are dancing. One-two-three, one-two-three.* George meticulously moved her panties aside and stroked her vagina with the back of his index finger. Sdia's eyes widened as she gripped onto the arms of the chair. She nervously began to scratch at the rips in the couch, pulling and scrabbling at cotton.

"I want my mommy!" she whined.

George frantically popped his head up and removed his hand from under her dress. "I told your ass your mama is working. She won't be back till later!" he said coldly, staring her in the eyes.

Sdia quickly looked down. She set her eyes on one of the sunflowers on her dress. *Don't blink, Sdia. Whatever you do, don't blink!* she coached herself as her eyes began to water.

"What the hell is wrong with you!" George shouted. Sdia gulped. "You know damn well your mama is at work!"

She took a deep breath as her bottom lip quivered. The longer she stared at the sunflower on her dress, the more her eyes tingled and filled with tears, causing the flower to transform into a blurry spot. Sdia bulged her eyes to avoid the tears from spilling. She clawed her fingernails into the arms of the couch, pulling and tugging at the loose pieces of cotton.

"Don't you go ripping that cotton out my chair!" George said, reaching up and snatching both of her hands from the arms of the chair.

Chapter 1

Sixteen years later . . .

"People act like they're doing God a favor by coming to church!" Pastor Jones shouted into the microphone. "But what you fail to realize is that God doesn't need you; you need God!" he stated boldly as he grabbed the microphone from its holder and walked down the stairs. "You see, that's the problem with folks these days. They think they're too good for God! Well, let me tell you … You ain't nothing without God!"

Sdia sat in the third row at Mount Calvary Baptist Church, shaking her head from side to side. *Feels like Pastor is talking to me! I needed to be here today to hear the Word.* She watched Pastor Jones as he made his way across the stage, removed the small white handkerchief from his suit jacket, and wiped his forehead. "God created you, and what do you do to show your appreciation?" His voice cracked. "I'll tell you what you do; you turn around and worship another human being. You show your gratitude by putting all your trust, love, and time into man, when all you need to do is call on your Lord and Savior, Jesus Christ!" he concluded, high-pitched.

"Man didn't wake you up this morning; man didn't save you in your time of need; man didn't send his only begotten son to forgive you for your sins; God did!" He stomped and jumped around in circles at the altar as the congregation stood to their feet and rejoiced with praise, shouting, "Hallelujah!"

Sdia lifted her head toward the ceiling and closed her eyes. "Hallelujah! Hallelujah! Hallelujah!" she sobbed as tears slowly fell from her eyes. Whimpers emerged from the pit of her stomach causing her body to jerk. *Please help me God. Please heal my heart Father-God. Please!* Her heart pounded in her chest; if she wanted she could have counted each beat. "Thank you Jesus. Thank you Father- God. Thank you Lord!" The pastor softly chanted into the microphone, and the organ played on cue as a young, slender gentleman emerged from the choir singing "I Need You Now" by Smokey Norful. Tears continued to spill from her eyes soaking her cheeks. Her eyes remained closed as her body rocked from side to side rhythmically with the organ. Her weeps were masked by the choir sending her back in time seven months ago . . .

"Just let me explain," Sean had said, running behind Sdia as she stormed ahead of him toward the restaurant's exit.

"Explain what?" Sdia yelled. "There ain't shit you can tell me!"

"I swear she's lying! Please believe me. She must be drunk or something," he pleaded, reaching for her arm. "I don't know what she's talking about!"

"Yeah, okay," she screamed, snatching her arm away and barging through the exit doors.

"I swear to God she's lying!" Sean said, now practically on her heels.

"Excuse me, sir?" their waiter called, running behind them. "Your receipt and change," he said, holding out their receipt and two crisp twenties.

"Keep the change." Sean waved without turning back.

Sdia's feet padded on the wet concrete as she quickly ran across the congested Manhattan streets. The cold winter rain lightly fell from the sky, frizzing her freshly straightened hair. "Shit. I need a taxi," she murmured, holding her clutch above her head with one hand and flagging down a taxi with the other.

"Sdia!" Sean called out as he ran across the street toward her. "Where are you going?"

"Stay the fuck away from me!" she shouted, turning and slapping him across the face with her purse, catching the attention of a pedestrian.

Sean grabbed her by the arm. "I swear on my dead grandmother I don't know what she's talking about!" he screeched. "I don't even know who that is."

"Get the fuck off me!" Sdia shouted, pulling away.

"Calm down. You're making a scene." Sean nervously looked around; the last thing he wanted was to catch the attention of a NYPD officer.

"I don't give a shit!" Sdia reached up, clawing his chin and lips with her stiletto-shaped fingernails. "You're full of shit!" She violently shoved him in the face; Sean's head jerked back. "Stay away from me!" she roared.

"You're bugging out." He slowly released her grip.

"*I'm* bugging out?" She quickly charged him like a bull.

"How the fuck am I the one bugging out when you're the one who had some random broad who clearly knows you, approaching you while we're out celebrating our so-called anniversary and saying 'Oooh, I'm telling!'"

Sean took a deep breath, placed both hands his hands in his pocket, and looked down at the wet pavement.

Sdia balled up her fist and began pacing back and forth. "I swear to God I should punch you in your face! I gotta get out of here!"

"I'm telling you that I don't know what that crazy bitch is talking about. She was probably drunk or something. First of all, did you see that bitch's lace front? The fucking hairline was on her forehead! How the fuck are you going to believe a bitch as black as tar wearing a cheap ass fake wig? I swear on my dead grandmother . . . I don't know why she would say that. Baby, please!" He grabbed her by the hand and softly kissed it. "I love you, and I would never do anything to hurt you or put our relationship in jeopardy!"

Sdia looked down at the ground. "Sean, please do not lie to me." He gently stroked both of her thighs.

"Baby, I'm not. Look, it's raining, it's cold, and we're both getting wet. Let's go home and put all of this behind us," he said, pulling her closer.

Slowly, Sdia raised her head and placed both hands on the side of his face. "Sean, look me in the eyes and tell me the truth."

Gently, he took her hands into his own and kissed them. "I love you, and you mean the world to me. Let's just go back to my place and—" Screeching tires approached, and he quickly glanced over to the street. "Oh shit!" he shouted, pushing Sdia aside.

"Sean?" Sdia called out into the darkness. He shooed her away as he ran toward the black 2019 Honda Civic, recklessly pulling up onto the curb. "Sean!" Sdia shouted. "What the fuck is going on!" a female shouted as the driver's door burst open.

"Let me explain," Sean replied, as the woman emerged wearing a Pink Victoria's Secret sweat suit, brown leather jacket, and brown suede UGGS. Honey-complexioned and about five-five, with very wide hips and thighs. Her hair was cut short; she slightly favored Halle Berry.

"Tina, calm down and let me explain." Sean's voice trembled as he rushed around to the driver's side.

"No, fuck that! You said it was over between y'all!" the woman shouted, pointing to Sdi.

"Tina, please just get back in the car," he begged, holding the woman by her shoulders and shoving her into the car.

Slowly, Sdia approached the vehicle. "What the hell is going on?" She moved her neck from side to side for a better view of the female, but the open driver's door made it impossible for her to get a full view.

"Sdia, stay over there!" Sean demanded, with his hand out.

"I wish she would come over here!" Tina snarled. "I'ma bust her ass."

"Sean, who is this hoodrat?" Sdia frowned.

"Hoodrat?" Tina roared. "Oh, hell no! Let me go! Let me go!" she said, wildly waving her arms, trying to break free from Sean's grip.

"Calm the fuck down!" Sean grabbed her by the arms. Get in the motherfucking car!" He violently shoved her back into the car, reached across her body, and snatched the keys from the ignition. "And don't get out!" he said, slamming the door.

Sdia placed her hand over heart. "Oh my God!" she said, hunching over as dinner from that evening resurfaced, exploding from her mouth and nose.

Sean quickly ran over, "Sdia, you okay?" he asked, kneeling. He gently rubbed her back with one hand and wiped the tears from his eyes with the other. Sdia sobbed uncontrollably as the rain fell ruthlessly from the sky onto the pavement, diluting her vomit. She weakly moved the vomited splattered pieces of hair from the side of her mouth.

"Get the fuck off of me, Sean!" she shouted, pulling away as he remained lowered toward the ground. "Stay the fuck away from me!"

"Baby, I'm sorry." Sean sniffled as tears spilled from his eyes. "I-I gotta go," he said, fumbling with the car keys, twirling them around his index finger.

***

The jingling of the church's tambourine snapped Sdia back into reality. *I can't believe he left me!* Tears rolled down the side of her cheeks and into her ears.

"That's right, praise Him! Let it out and praise Him!" the elderly woman sitting beside her said. She tilted her head back and joined Sdia. "Thank you, Lord!" she shouted, staring at the ceiling. "Hallelujah!" she hollered, taking Sdia by the hand as tears fell from her own eyes.

Sdia opened her eyes, scrunched her nose, and looked at the woman. "Excuse me," she said, respectfully pulling her hand away.

The woman peeked at Sdia from the corner of her eyes. "Are you okay, dear?" she asked, opening both eyes.

With the back of her hand, Sdia wiped her eyes. "Yes. I just need some fresh air."

"Pardon me." Her voice cracked as she rose to her feet. "Excuse me." She made her way through the crowded aisles with her head hung low.

Sdia fanned her hand in front of her face. *God forgive me, but I gotta get out of here.*

"Excuse me," she said, briskly walking past an usher. She forcefully pushed the heavy metal double doors open, and the thick, hot, muggy air instantly latched onto her skin. She let out a sigh of relief that no one was outside of the church. She took advantage of the opportunity and permitted the welled up tears to freely roll down her cheeks. She bent down to remove the four-inch Gucci sandals from her feet and placed them under her right arm. *I just want to go home*, she thought as she quickly walked across the crowded parking lot, licking the falling salty tears from the top of her lip.

"Asshole!" she said, jerking the car door open and tossing her shoes into the backseat. "Son-of-a- bitch gonna break up with me!" she whimpered while starting the ignition. "Two and a half years of my life down the fucking drain! I should block my number and call his ass." She snatched her iPhone from her purse and looked at the blank screen and hesitantly dialed his number. *Let go and let God*, she remembered the pastor's words. She paused and glanced out of the window. *What's wrong with me? It's 7:45 in the morning, and I'm sitting in the car when I should be in church. I left service early because of him?* She looked down at her phone and let out a deep sigh. "I know exactly who to call," she said, deleting the numbers on her screen.

"Hello?" her mother Sharon answered groggily.

"I miss him," Sdia quickly blurted out.

"Shouldn't you be in church?" Sharon asked. "Yeah, I should be, but this is really annoying me."

"Sdia, we can talk about this tomorrow when you get here. You really need to be in church."

"I don't understand how he could do this." "Didn't you hear what I just said?"

"Yeah, I hear you, but I'm not thinking about service right now! I came outside to call you, Ma, not to talk about church."

"Look!" Sharon raised her tone. "God is more important than some nigga. See, you already have me yelling. And I don't want to awake your father," she whispered.

"Sorry, Ma."

"Mmm hmm," Sharon replied.

"Ma, I'm sad. Say something to make me feel better." "Sdia, you can't keep on tormenting yourself over his

decision. Besides, hasn't it been almost a year since you two broke up? You need to let it go!" Sharon whispered.

"No, it hasn't been a year! It's only been seven months, two weeks, and five days."

"Okay, okay, don't kill me," Sharon replied in her normal tone, noticing the chord she struck."

"I just don't get it, Ma." Sdia sighed.

"Why do I have to keep telling you the same thing? You have so much going for yourself. You're—"

"Smart, beautiful, and independent. I can have any man I want. Why do I allow that loser to occupy so much space in my brain? Right, Ma?" A beat passed between them. "Thanks for the typical pep talk. Well, if I'm all of those things, why did he cheat? Why doesn't he see those qualities in me?" Sdia asked, a blink away from more tears. "Because maybe they're not for him to see. What's important is that you see those things!" Sharon sighed. "I am getting so tired of telling you the same thing, Dia. If you don't see these things in yourself, then no man is going to treat you the way you deserve to be treated!"

"I know, Ma. I know. It's just that I really wish I could get even with him!"

"What did I tell you, Dia? You don't have to worry about hurting anyone because people don't get away with doing shit. Remember, only hurt people hurt people, and his day is coming."

"They're probably having sex right now as we speak," Sdia added.

"So what if they are! Who gives a shit? I wouldn't want him touching me, especially after he slept with someone else."

"I don't want him to touch me!" Sdia lied.

"Good. There's no sense in sitting there making yourself depressed over something that is clearly out of your control!"

"I know, but—" Sdia replied.

"Listen," Sharon interrupted. "If it's meant for you and Sean to be together and God knows I pray it isn't; it will be!" She paused. "The only thing you should be worried about is getting back in that church and preparing for your trip tomorrow; anything else is minute, especially a damn man—a lying, cheating one at that!"

"I know, Ma."

"I'm glad you know. Now get your tail back in that church; you're on the Lord's time, and I need to start breakfast!"

"Okay, I love you, Ma."

"Uh-huh, love you too. I swear you gotta get it together, girl. I can't keep telling you the same thing over and over again. Anyway, call me when service is over."

Sdia placed her phone back into her purse and grabbed her shoes from the backseat. *Let go and let God* she thought, as she stepped from her vehicle and back into the blazing sun. She slowly walked up the small path leading to the church and up the steep stairs. Once inside she looked around until she spotted the elderly woman she had been sitting next to and maneuvered her way back to her seat.

"Are you okay dear?" the woman asked. Sdia nodded and looked up at the image of Jesus on the stained glass ceiling.

I'm not gonna let you fight Tina! Sdia, she's pregnant with my baby! Sean's words resonated in her head. *Wait... what! Pregnant? Baby?* Sdia didn't fight back her tears this time. Instead she allowed them to flow.

"That's right, baby. Let it out. Just let go and let God," the elderly woman whispered.

I still can't believe he has a baby now! Sdia thought.

TAHANEE

WAHIDA CLARK PRESENTS

One Last Deadly Play

A Novel By
FLO ANTHONY

This is a work of fiction. Names, characters, places, and incidents either are the product of the author's imagination or are used fictitiously, and any resemblance to actual persons, living or dead, business establishments, events, or locales is entirely coincidental.

Wahida Clark Presents Publishing, LLC
60 Evergreen Place
Suite 904
East Orange, New Jersey 07018
1(866)-910-6920
www.wclarkpublishing.com

Copyright 2016 © by Flo Anthony
All rights reserved. This book, or parts thereof, may not be reproduced in any form without permission.

ISBN 13-digit 978-1-936649-05-1
ISBN 10-digit 19366490550
eBook ISBN 9781936649198

Library of Congress Catalog Number
1. Urban, Romance, Suspense, Gossip, Football, New York City, African-American, Street Lit – Fiction

Cover design and layout by Nuance Art, LLC
Book interior design by www.aCreativeNuance.com
Contributing Editors: Linda Wilson and R. Hamilton

Printed in United States

Chapter One

Columbus

Columbus wished he had a clue to his true identity or where he really came from. The sole doctor on Crooked Island told Columbus that he suffered from something called "traumatic amnesia," a condition that must have occurred as a result of his near drowning. Some fishermen, who are part of the 350 residents on the island, pulled him out of the ocean half a decade ago. Since he had no recollection of ever even having a name, the guys decided to call him Columbus Isley after Christopher Columbus, who sailed down the side of the island in 1492.

Christopher Columbus called the island the Fragrant Isles. Legend said it was because of the refreshing scent of the cascarilla tree's bark, also called Eluethera bark. Thus, he had been named Columbus Isley, with his surname deriving from Isles. One of the fishermen who rescued Columbus said it was the last name of a famous singing group made up of brothers in the United States. Columbus couldn't remember having any brothers, but he did have a vague feeling that he had known a couple of men who looked like him.

As he'd done each and every morning at the crack of dawn for the last five years, Columbus Isley prepared breakfast for the guests at Morning Glory, a small lodge with only twelve rooms. He fingered the sparkling bottle-like emblem that hung from a thick gold chain around his neck after cracking the last egg. His friends had explained that it was a replica of a bat used to play an American game called baseball. The lodge provided only one television inside the bar, and it only got six local stations, so Columbus still had no idea what the game was. There was nothing even vaguely familiar about it to him.

Aside from the few tourists who actually traveled to the secret community located 583 miles off the Florida coast and the residents on the island, Columbus hadn't had much contact with the outside world. Only one telephone was in the lodge's office, and most residents depended on generators for electricity. There was no use of credit cards and only one bank. The mail boat came once a week, and only one flight arrived and departed twice weekly at Colonel Hill, a 4,000- foot airstrip on the southwest portion of the island.

Columbus, a black man with skin the color of honey and wild, curly, salt and pepper gray hair, piercing green eyes and the body of an African warrior, managed to catch the eye of a twenty-three-year-old white woman who originally came to Crooked Island accompanied by an addiction coach to overcome a problem with heroin. She also wanted to escape the fast-paced, drug-fueled modeling world in New York City and get her life and mental and physical well-being back.

Over the past couple of years, Ariel and Columbus had become very attached. One thing he remembered was how to make love to a woman, and how good his penis felt every time he entered her vagina. Just thinking about Ariel made Columbus's loins throb. He smiled. His lady was due back on Crooked Island on today's plane. Soon, they would be lying on a secluded beach, lost in a sea of lust.

His thoughts must have conjured her up. As Columbus got the coffee going, two milky-white arms wrapped around his waist. The beautiful woman's delicious smelling perfume engulfed him. He turned, pulled her to him, and then deeply kissed Ariel Pembrough, a bootylicious blonde with skin soft to the touch.

"You're back," Columbus said with a grin.

"Yes, I am," purred the supermodel, as her sky blue eyes glittered up at him. She stepped out of her yellow maxi sundress. She was panty-less.

Quickly locking the kitchen door, Columbus lifted her up on the counter and spread her legs. In the heat of passion he pulled his shorts down, then thrust his manhood into Ariel. These two lovers became one, losing themselves into each other.

"Well, that was a nice welcome," said Ariel as Columbus gently wiped her clean with a warm cloth as if she were a baby. She slipped her dress back on. Kissing her lightly on the lips, Columbus noticed the newspaper sticking out of her purse.

"What are you reading?"

"Oh, just an article about this wild murder case that's about to go on trial in Los Angeles today. It caught my attention because the guy in the photo looks like a lighter version of you. I thought he could be related to you or something. It says his name is Rolondo Jemison. It also involves the gossip columnist, Valerie Rollins. She's a friend of my mom's." Both names jarred something in his head. Columbus looked at the picture of the man. Sharp pains made him think his head was about to explode. A massive pounding in his chest quickly followed.

"Arrghhhhh," he groaned as he collapsed on to the floor.

Like what you've read?
VISIT THE FOLLOWING LINK TO ORDER NOW
http://amzn.to/2tl3NLb

WAHIDA CLARK PRESENTS

THUGGZ VALENTINE

BY
WAHIDA CLARK

This is a work of fiction. Names, characters, places, and incidents either are the product of the author's imagination or are used fictitiously, and any resemblance to actual persons, living or dead, business establishments, events, or locales are entirely coincidental.

Wahida Clark Presents Publishing
60 Evergreen Place
Suite 904A
East Orange, New Jersey 07018
1(866)-910-6920
www.wclarkpublishing.com

Copyright 2015 © by Wahida Clark
All rights reserved. This book, or parts thereof, may not be reproduced in any form without permission.

Library of Congress Cataloging-In-Publication Data:
Thuggz Valentine by Wahida Clark
ISBN 13-digit 978-19366496-3-1 (paper)
ISBN 10-digit 1936649632 (paper)
ISBN 13-digit 978-1-936649-18-1
ISBN 10-digit 1-936649-18-7
LCCN: 2015910467

1. New Jersey- 2. Thug Life 3. Murder- 4. African American- Fiction- 5. Urban Fiction- 6. Natural Born Killers- 7. Gangster Disciples- 8. Prescription Drugs- 9. HIV- 10. AIDS-

Cover design and layout by Nuance Art, LLC Book design by www.aCreativeNuance.com
Sr. Editors Linda Wilson, Latoya Smith and Keisha Caldwell
Proofreader Rosalind Hamilton

Printed in USA

THE END
Bless and Ebony

CHAPTER ONE

February 14
6:15 p.m.

"Thuggz Valentine, mutherfuckaz!"

The ground shook from the explosion.

Kabooooooom!

The blast rattled the ground like an earthquake, igniting cars and SUVs, shattering store windows, knocking out the power, and setting off car alarms within a two-block downtown Newark radius. Several bystanders were killed, including a few police officers who'd had the two suspects surrounded, as well as every person inside the overturned bus, which was the source of the blast. People thought it was a terrorist attack.

It wasn't.

It was a standing ovation for Bless and Ebony. They embraced death on their own terms. They lived their last day on the edge and to the fullest. Even though it was filled with murder and mayhem.

Three minutes earlier . . .
6:12 p.m.
"Fuck y'all!" Bless managed to yell out, despite the burning sensation of the bullet wounds and a natural sense of impending doom. His head rested on Ebony's lap while her back leaned against the underbelly of the overturned bus.

Ebony stroked his head. "Shhh baby. Save your energy."

Muffled cries and yells of anguish echoed from the passengers trapped inside. There was no escape. The bus had landed on the door side, destining everyone inside to a fiery fate. Desperate, the imprisoned riders beat furiously on sealed windows, too dazed and hurt by the crash to even come close to shattering them. Their hysterical eyes gazed at all the police surrounding them in a half moon formation. Officers shielded themselves behind open doors with automatic weapons, pistols, and shotguns all trained on Bless and Ebony. High above, a police helicopter hovered.

"It's over." Bless closed his eyes.

"No, baby, not yet. Remember what you said? Real gangstas never give up," she reminded him.

He forced a smile onto his lips. "You . . . you, could've saved yourself."

With tears running down her cheeks, she stroked his face. "Today has been the best day of my life. Before you, I didn't know what it really meant to be free. I am feeling totally alive. Anything after this would be a disappointment. I love you, Bless," she expressed, but she knew he hadn't heard her. She felt his body convulse, tighten, and then relax. She knew he was gone. She had been speaking to his soul. A soul she knew much deeper than even she was conscious of. Ebony held back every tear but one, which escaped down her cheek. She closed Bless's lifeless eyes with two fingers that resembled the peace sign, and then laid her gun on her leg. A tall, black detective stepped out of the police mob with his arms raised. He advanced slowly.

"Listen to me, Miss. Please. This can all end peacefully. I want to walk you out of this alive," he pleaded.

"Believe me . . . I plan to," Ebony said.

"That's good. Very good," he replied, missing the significance of her tone.

Ebony reached into Bless's pocket and pulled out his crumpled pack of Newport's and matches. "Don't shoot!

Don't shoot! It's just a cigarette!" she bellowed at the itchy trigger-fingered officers.

Just a cigarette . . . She didn't smoke.

She put it in her mouth, lit it up, then inhaled a satisfying stream of smoke. When she exhaled, all the fear that she was harboring vanished.

"Now, I'm going to ask you to toss the gun over, okay?" She inhaled. "Not yet."

He shook his head. "No! I said now! Look around you." She did.

"It's over! There is nowhere to go!" he warned her.

Ebony glanced at all the stone-faced police squinting through scopes, with her head in the crosshairs. She took in all the gawking downtown onlookers, all while hearing the stifled cries of the people on the bus. And lastly, she looked up at the beautiful blue sky.

"Yeah, you right. There's nowhere to go . . ." she remarked, and then struck another match. "But up."

She and the cop exchanged glances. Yet, he strained at the match. The realization hit him when he saw the leaking gas from the overturned bus pooling in the street and settling like a beached whale. His brown eyes widened in horror, taking in the implications of the lit match.

"Nooooo!" he yelled. But it was too late . . .

"Thuggz Valentine, mutherfuckaz!" she screamed, laughing as if life was one big joke.

Then . . . she tossed the match.

Like what you've read?
VISIT THE FOLLOWING LINK TO ORDER NOW
http://amzn.to/2ufz5Y5

WAHIDA CLARK PRESENTS

T.H.O.T

BY
ALAH ADAMS

This is a work of fiction. Names, characters, places, and incidents either are the product of the author's imagination or are used fictitiously, and any resemblance to actual persons, living or dead, business establishments, events, or locales is entirely coincidental.

Wahida Clark Presents Publishing, LLC
60 Evergreen Place
Suite 904A
East Orange, New Jersey 07018
1 (866)-910-6920
www.wclarkpublishing.com

Copyright 2016 © by Alah Adams
All rights reserved. This book, or parts thereof, may not be reproduced in any form without permission.

ISBN 13-digit 978-1-936649-25-9
ISBN 10-digit 193664925X eBook
ISBN 97819366490-6-8

Library of Congress Catalog Number 2017904229
1. Urban Life 2. Suspense 3. Drugs 4. Hustle, 5. New York City 6. African-Americans-Fiction 7.THOT

Cover design and layout by Nuance Art, LLC
Book interior design by www.aCreativeNuance.com
Contributing Editors: Linda Wilson and R. Hamilton

Printed in United States

Prologue

Vinny hid in the bedroom closet of the plush condo he purchased for Chasity. Heart racing with anxiety, he opened the bottle of Oxycodone he held and popped two pills.

He shed tears as he listened to Torian pounding her vagina as if he were killing her.

"Oh my god!" Chasity screamed out in ecstasy. "You are the best! Keep fucking me!"

Furious, Vinny's chest heaved, and he couldn't control his jaw from grinding. His hand shook, almost causing him to drop his weapon and the pills. He shoved the bottle back into his pants pocket. *I can't believe this is happening. I trusted her with everything, and this is how she repays me.* Vinny cocked the .45 caliber ACP pistol. *I knew I should've listened to Rocco.* He sniffled. The effects of the powerful opiate was starting to kick in.

"What's that noise?" Torian asked, stopping mid-stroke after hearing a clicking of some kind. "Sounds like somebody's in the closet." Torian dismounted Chasity and grabbed his pants where he'd concealed his 9-millimeter. Before he could grip his weapon, Vinny rushed out of the closet busting shots.

Bang! Bang! Bang!

The first shot hit Torian in his shoulder, pushing him two steps back. He fell to the floor about two feet from his 9- millimeter. He lay there not making a sound, pretending to be unconscious, yet inching his hand toward his gun. The other two bullets landed in the headboard right by Chasity's head.

"Vinny!" she screamed and flinched, holding her arms up in the air. "Baby, please put the gun down . . . It's not what it looks like."

"That's all you have to say!" He looked at her with red teary eyes, seething in anger.

Bang!

He let off a shot right by her head. Tears streamed down Vinny's face. "I gave you *everything!* I took you from living in motels selling your ass, to a condo and a BMW! And this is how you repay me!" He lunged toward her as if to strike her with the butt of his gun.

She quickly guarded her head with her hands. "Wait! I can explain!" She forced a smile in an attempt to calm him down. "I don't want to hear it!" Vinny pointed the gun at Chasity. "I should kill you!"

Torian got his hand on his gun, but he didn't have a clear shot at Vinny because of the angle. Vinny moved closer to Chasity, putting the gun to her head, which gave Torian the perfect advantage. Just as Torian's index finger pressed on the trigger, Vinny saw him in his peripheral, turned, and let off two shots in rapid succession.

Bang! Bang!

One of the shots hit Torian in his chest, but not before Torian let off three shots at the same time. Two shots hit Vinny in his neck; the third shot pierced the closet door. He slumped to the ground while gurgling on his blood. Both men lay on the floor, gravely injured.

Chasity stood viewing the carnage. Vinny tried to use his hands to squeeze the wounds in his neck to stop the blood from flowing. It was too late; in three minutes his hands unclasped his neck, and he lay peacefully still. Vinny was dead.

She slowly turned to look at Torian as he lay motionless with his eyes wide open staring right at Chasity. Instantly she turned her head and squeezed her eyelids as tight as she could. She opened them and turned back to the same horrific scene. The man she really loved was gone.

"This isn't real," she told herself. "Snap out of it!" She couldn't believe what had just happened.

At that moment, her mind had been stripped of its ability to reason. Disoriented, she gazed at both bodies as if they were illusions. Suffolk County police officers entering the room with their guns drawn, brought her out of her trance.

"Get on the floor with your hands behind your head!" the officer yelled.

Unresponsive, Chasity stood there stark naked.

The officer, seeing her blank expression, realized she posed no immediate threat. Cautious, he moved toward her, took one of the blankets that lay on the king-sized bed and covered Chasity's body. The other officers looked at the two bodies on the floor. They glimpsed the .45 caliber ACP next to Vinny, and the 9-millimeter lying next to Torian.

The first officer put his gun away and grabbed Chasity by her shoulders. "Miss, are you all right?"

She remained upright but in a catatonic-like state, experiencing the effects of extreme shock.

After a half hour, the officer took her to a police vehicle, while the homicide squad combed over the scene. It was cut and dry: two men shot each other to death over a woman. It didn't take long for them to surmise the situation.

Still in shock, but no longer catatonic, Chasity was escorted to the precinct where she was placed in a small interrogation room. The officer helped her put clothes on before they left. Now she sat in the cold, gray room looking confused. The door suddenly opened, and in walked a tall, heavyset female with a detective badge hanging from her neck. Her black pantsuit and white button-down shirt fit her frame well.

"How are you doing? My name is Detective Jennifer Colon." She wore a serious expression as she glanced at the paperwork she held. "Miss Chasity Tommyson, that's you, right?"

Chasity met the detective's gaze for a moment before turning her head and looking at the wall. She took a few seconds before speaking. "Yes, that's me."

"Okay, Chasity. Can you tell me what happened today?" Detective Colon slammed the door and looked down at Chasity with disgust. Her long, dark hair fell over her face, hiding her curled lip and heated gaze. She moved her hair aside and stared at Chasity with unfriendly dark brown eyes before taking a seat.

Chasity's eyes widened, but they didn't blink. She seemed to be regressing into her guilty conscience.

"Take your time, take a deep breath," Detective Colon suggested. "If you want me to help you, I need you to tell me how this happened . . . from the beginning."

Slowly, Chasity took in a deep breath and let it out just as measured.

"It all started a year ago when I first met Vinny . . ."

Detective Colon pressed record on the mini video recorder that sat on a tripod. "Okay, take your time. Start from the beginning."

Chasity closed her eyes, but when she opened them she began speaking. "I'm not at all what I appear to be. I have deceived many men by using my looks and my body to lure them into my world of lust. The warning signs were all around me, telling me to stop, telling me that there was danger ahead. But I didn't listen, and now two men are dead. And it's all because of me."

Chasity paused and gazed into the camera wearing a slight smile.

* * * *

CHAPTER 1

A Sucker, With a Capital 'S!'

Bay Shore Motor Inn
Bay Shore Long Island, New York

Chasity

"*Middle fingers up / throw them hands high / middle fingers up/tell em boy bye/boy bye/I aint thinking bout you/Sorry/naw I aint sorry."* Chasity sang along with Beyonce to her new single 'Sorry' as it blasted on the radio.

"This is my new anthem! Because I really don't give a fuck about these niggas!" Chasity spoke with passion while she inhaled a huge blunt, then she passed it to Kat.

"My sentiments exactly!" Kat replied as she reached for the blunt and inhaled.

Scantily clad in red Victoria's Secret matching bra and panties, Chasity sat on the bed with her laptop open, checking her traps on the infamous "Front Page" website. Front Page was a way for tricks and 'hos to link up via the Internet. She liked to use the word *trap* to describe the way she enticed weak men into her web of deceit and pleasure. Chasity was a modern day call girl, a prostitute, otherwise known in the hood as a THOT, an acronym for 'That Ho Out There.'

"The day just started, and I already have three new traps lined up. At $250 apiece, that's $750 for about an hour's worth of work," Chasity said to Kat, her best friend and partner in crime.

"The way these tricks be coming so fast, you can cut that hour into thirty minutes worth of work." Kat inhaled the blunt and then passed it to Chasity.

"I got this one trick that fucks me for the whole hour! I think that nigga be on something before he comes here," Chasity responded.

The days of 'hos walking the strip trying to catch a date were a thing of the past. Nowadays these young thots knew how to use the Internet to their advantage by posting provocative pictures with an implied message. The tricks were up on the new technology, so they went on the sites looking for new 'hos to trick on. That cut out the pimp and the risk of being seen by detectives walking on the 'Thot Trot,' the blocks where primitive thots walked trying to catch a trap.

Chasity and Kat were two of the best 'thots' in Long Island. Both women were voluptuous with gorgeous faces. They were divas, so they always adorned their heads with expensive wigs, kept their toes and nails done, and wore the newest designer labels. They were known to frequent the VIP section in the hottest clubs, buying their own bottles, balling out!

Tall with big brown eyes, Chasity inherited a honey-brown complexion from her Puerto Rican mother and black father. Her pearly white teeth were esthetically pleasing to the eye. When she got dressed up, people often told her she resembled Beyoncé. She kept her stomach flat which made her firm, size 38D cups stand at attention. Chasity was a complete ten!

Kat was a bit shorter, but her ass wasn't. Ass for days, flat stomach, and a nice amount of tits, she was a little darker than Chasity, but people always mistook them for sisters. Chasity and Kat didn't see the resemblance, but they chalked it up to them being around each other so much that they started looking alike. As a team, they were like the dynamic duo.

"That's my number one trap texting me," Kat said when her phone went off. "He's here. I'm going to my room to take care of him."

"Okay, my trap should be here shortly. I'll see you for lunch," Chasity said.

"That sounds like a plan."

Kat went two rooms down. They always got rooms close to each other for safety. Being that they didn't have pimps to protect them, they both kept revolvers close to them at all times. In the past, they had been violated by tricks who knew they didn't have pimps.

Shortly after Kat left the room, Chasity's new trap knocked on the door. She knew it was him, so she sprayed herself with Chanel No. 5 before answering. Her motto was "Go above and beyond to please" to ensure that her traps stayed loyal. She answered the door in her Victoria's Secret undergarments.

"Hi. Vinny, right?" she asked, showing her perfect rows of white teeth.

"Yes, I'm Vinny. You're Cherry?" he asked in a nervous tone. *Wow! This chick is fucking beautiful! I hit the jackpot!* Vinny was stuck in thought standing in the doorway.

She quickly glanced at him from head to toe before inviting him in. "You can come in and make yourself comfortable."

Short, fat, and Italian with slick, black hair, Vinny wasn't quite the looker, but he was very charming. He possessed a gentleman-like quality that made him attractive to women. He was like a knight in shining armor, without the shining armor.

Chasity had a sixth sense for men who were enamored by her. Her 'sucker for love' meter dinged off the charts with this new guy. At first sight she could tell he was smitten by her beauty. She was a pro at tempting men, so she knew exactly how to handle him.

"So, Vinny, what do you do for a living?" she batted her light brown eyes.

"I'm in the construction business." Vinny stared at her in awe.

"Oh, I see . . . construction. Are you a foreman?" she asked.

"No. I own a construction business with my family." Vinny kept rubbing his hands together in an attempt to calm his nerves. *Get it together, Vin!* he thought.

"It must be nice to work with your family."

"Not all the time, but it beats working for some Joe Schmo."

Chasity stared in his eyes and he got weak. She moved closer and he almost jumped. Normally, she would ask for money up front, but she was playing him all the way to the bank. She smelled money like a shark smells plasma.

"Relax, I'm not going to bite you. Unless you tell me to." She smiled, and Vinny seemed to unwind a bit.

Getting right down to business, Chasity unbuckled his belt and pants and pulled his penis out. Vinny almost freaked out, breathing heavily. Immediately, she took him into her mouth as if her life depended on it. The force with which she sucked his penis made Vinny's toes curl in seconds. She felt his sperm swelling up in his balls early, so she slurped with more ferociousness.

"Oh my God!" Vinny yelled out in ecstasy. "I'm coming!" "Mmmmm! It tastes so good!" Chasity said as she lapped up his semen.

Vinny's eyes rolled around in his head. "You're the best! I mean that."

"Never had any complaints."

"No, really. No woman has ever made me come that fast from sucking my dick before." Vinny took out five 100 dollar bills. "I know you said it was only $250, but you were so good I'm giving you double!"

I got him! Hook, line, and sucker! "Aww, you don't have to do that. You're so sweet, Vinny."

"No, I want you to take it. I want to see you every day if that's possible?" He panted as sweat beads dotted his forehead and nose, looking at her like a puppy that needed attention from its master.

"Of course you can, silly!" Chasity laughed. "You're so funny!"

". . . Can we just cuddle for a minute?" Vinny knew that was a weird question.

"Sure, baby. Take your clothes off and get under the covers. You still have about fifty minutes left."

Vinny did as he was told. He curled up and went to sleep with Chasity as if she were his wife. He was officially open. *Damn this nigga hooked already, and I didn't even throw this tight, wet pussy on him yet.* Chasity let him sleep for an hour, then she woke him.

"Wake up, sleepy head. Time to go."

"Damn, I was out of it." Vinny got up and put his clothes on. "So, I'll see you tomorrow at the same time?"

"If that's what you want, honey. I'll be here waiting for you, baby." She kissed him on the cheek.

Vinny finally left, and she watched him walk away to see what model car he drove. When he sat comfortably in a new jet black BMW 650i convertible, she knew she'd hit the jackpot. *Everything about Vinny screams money. And I want it all!*

Just as Vinny was leaving, Chasity got a text from her next client: *I'm pulling in right now.*

Chasity: *Okay, I'm ready.*

She went to the bathroom and rinsed her mouth out with mouthwash and brushed her teeth. As she was finishing up, there was a knock on the door.

With the same smile as before, she answered it. "Hi, Tommy. Come in and make yourself comfortable."

Tommy was a regular, and he wasn't a two-minute man. He was smart enough to pop a Viagra before his weekly appointments. Also, Tommy wasn't rich. He was just a truck driver with an appetite for young thots. Every week he would spend his hard earned money on one hour of pleasure.

Tall and light-skinned, the older black man had been married twice and divorced twice. Although he came equipped with a ten-inch penis, his last girlfriend cheated on him with his best friend, and that's when he decided to deal with women like Chasity and call it a day. For him it was less headaches and no commitment, that's what he enjoyed most about the situation.

Tommy didn't waste any time. Chasity knew that Tommy came to put in work, so she prepared her mind for the task of getting fucked hard. He took his clothes off and put his stiff penis in her mouth and shoved it down her throat. She moaned in protest, but she didn't stop him from manhandling her. There was something about his roughness that Chasity enjoyed. He didn't treat her like the doll she appeared to be. Tommy treated her like the thot he knew she was. And Chasity loved it.

For fifty-five minutes straight, Tommy pummeled her vagina before ejaculating and leaving her sore. "I'll see you next week, same time." Tommy was a man of few words. He was dressed and out the door minutes after he was done.

Chasity had twenty minutes before her next appointment, and she wasn't ready. She dragged her sore body to the bathroom and took a long, hot shower. As she rubbed her vagina, she thought about her first trick, Vinny. *I knew Vinny was a breadwinner! What if I can entice Vinny to the point where he'll just take care of me, and I don't have to be fucking like this for money? It would be nice to be taken care of for a change.* She became so engrossed in her thoughts that she lost track of time.

There was a knock on the door. Her next trap was on time. "Hold on, I'm coming!" she shouted from the shower as she got out and dried off. *Got to get this money. It's all in a day's work.* Chasity opened the door.

"Hi Paul. Come in and make yourself comfortable."

The quick arm movement in her peripheral disrupted Chasity's recollection. Detective Colon paused the video. "So, you met Vinny on the Front Page website." A beat passed before she spoke again. "I'm going to do you a favor."

"What's that?"

"I'm not going to arrest you for prostitution. Let's just pretend like I don't know anything about that. I'll erase the whole first part when we're done, so we both won't get into hot water."

Detective Colon pushed record on the video. "Continue." *Murderous slut! You just couldn't keep your fucking cunt- hole closed!*

Like what you've read?
VISIT THE FOLLOWING LINK TO ORDER NOW
http://amzn.to/2t9fZTT

WAHIDA CLARK PRESENTS

Black Senate
Sneak Peek

By
Zaid Za'hid

This is a work of fiction. Names, characters, places, and incidents either are the product of the author's imagination or are used fictitiously, and any resemblance to actual persons, living or dead, business establishments, events, or locales are entirely coincidental.

Wahida Clark Presents Publishing
60 Evergreen Place
Suite 904A
East Orange, New Jersey 07018
1(866)-910-6920
www.wclarkpublishing.com

Copyright 2017 © by Zaid Zah'id
All rights reserved. This book, or parts thereof, may not be reproduced in any form without permission.

Library of Congress Cataloging-In-Publication Data:

ISBN 13-digit 978-1944992-54-5 (paperback)
ISBN 13-digit 978-1944992569 (ebook)
ISBN 13-digit: 978-1944992552 (Hardback)
LCCN: 2017904233

1. Crime 2. Drug Trafficking- 3. African Americans-Fiction- 4. Urban Fiction- 5. Mafia- 6. Chicago-

Cover design and layout by Nuance Art, LLC
Book design by NuanceArt@aCreativeNuance.com
Edited by Linda Wilson

Printed in USA

I
PENITENTIARY CHANCES
CHAPTER ONE

Dressed in all black, Malachi, YaYa, and Jerusalem sat around a chestnut brown table loading and checking their automatic weapons. The crew had graduated from just young hustlers to controlling their own turf. If it came down to it, they killed for their respect with no hesitation. They quickly got a reputation and a name for themselves. Some even called them the BBB—Bad Black Brothas.

Inside the rundown apartment, one of the most notorious projects in Chicago, they passed the blunt around as Tupac's song, "Get Money" played in the background. Jerusalem recited on beat, ". . . today I make a killing . . ." He stopped rapping so they could go over their plan to rob First National Bank.

If they pulled off the heist, they would have enough money to increase their drug supply and expand their organization. This would eliminate some of their competitors. The old heads in the drug game were not showing Jerusalem and his crew any love. They hated to see the young soldiers moving up so rapidly, and they wouldn't let Jerusalem score from them. When they did let Jerusalem score, they almost doubled the prices on the product, making it hard for him to profit. So Jerusalem came up with a plan. With an inside connection, he, along with his crew, planned to hold up one of the largest banks in the city. If he possessed more money, he could bypass the old heads and one day get close enough to kill them all. This was the day they were to put their plan in action.

Jerusalem turned toward Malachi and said, "Remember, your job is to hold off the guard, but without killing him."

Malachi, with dreads that barely sat on his shoulders, responded, "If anyone flinches, I'm shooting. I'm not hesitating to plug their ass."

"Just don't get trigger happy, 'cause I know you have a hair trigger finger. If it's not necessary to commit a murder in this robbery, then don't do it. Our whole mission is to go in, get this money, and come out. We got two minutes to do this from the time we enter the bank," Jerusalem said.

"Where Pinky's yellow ass at?" YaYa asked.

"You know she's always late. That bitch will be late for her own funeral because her stupid ass would be trying to put her own make-up on," Malachi said.

They all laughed but got quiet when they heard the secret knock—two taps and a pause then one tap and a pause and three taps. Malachi jumped up and opened the door. "Bitch, where you been?"

"You think stealing a SUV is easy," Pinky, the streetwise and curvaceous eighteen year old said while rolling her neck with lots of attitude. "Jerusalem told me specifically to get a dark SUV. Motherfucker, I had my girl drive me all over Chimney Hills this morning before I found one." Her role in the heist was only to be the get-a-way driver.

Jerusalem eyed the 5-feet 5-inches tall, big, emerald eyed beauty in the tight fitting jeans she loved to wear to show off her body. Her heart-shaped head was filled with long, dark curly hair drawn up into a ponytail.

"You're looking beautiful, ma," he said. "What you have on is perfect? 'Cause you're supposed to look like an ordinary patron, a beautiful woman behind the wheel. When we enter the car, we don't want you to do no speeding. Drive the speed limit, because we're going to duck down where it looks like you're the only one in the SUV.

"YaYa, your role is to make sure that all the customers and workers in the bank are under control. Whatever you do, don't let a motherfucka get to their cell phone."

"I got you," YaYa responded.

While talking, they loaded their guns, ski masks, and gloves into one duffel bag.

Jerusalem asked Pinky, "You strapped already?"

Her full-sized, pink lips moved as she replied, "Yes, I keep my man with me." She patted her small waistline to indicate the weapon was securely hidden. With the curves she carried, every hustler in the neighborhood attempted to get their hands on Pinky. Men drooled over her every time they saw her thick hips and ass like Serena Williams.

They exited the project doors.

An hour later, after casing the area one last time, Pinky pulled the SUV in front of the bank. Jerusalem looked around the area. "Go," he said.

Malachi, pulling the black Spider-Man mask over his head, was the first to exit the SUV. He held the AK-47 assault rifle out as he entered the bank doors. YaYa followed suit, holding a .357 Smith and Wesson with extra bullets around his waist. When he walked, his shirt swayed, revealing the weapon. Jerusalem patted his pocket, confirming he had four extra clips in each one. He tightened his Spider-Man mask down under his chin and extended his .45 automatic weapon as he entered the bank last.

"Everybody get the fuck down!" Malachi yelled. "Don't nobody fucking move!"

It looked as if the security guard was contemplating a move. Malachi immediately put the gun to the white security guard's head and said, "Motherfucka, don't even flinch. If you do, I won't hesitate to put a bullet in your fuckin' head." YaYa yelled out, "Down on the floor, now! Keep your hands visible where I can see them." He waved the gun near the customers to show he meant business. Some of the

customers wailed, but they all obeyed.

Jerusalem jumped over the bank counter with the duffle bag. "You three, on the floor. Now!"

The three women crowded together and whimpered. One sounded like she was hyperventilating as they bent down and got on the floor. Jerusalem ignored them and pointed the gun at the bank manager. "You too."

Only one cashier remained standing, and she was the one Jerusalem knew.

"A minute and forty-five seconds!" YaYa yelled near the frightened customers.

Jerusalem turned his attention to the cashier and pointed the gun to the side of her head and said, "Bitch, you know what to do. Take me to the money."

Instead of Jerusalem taking her to the cashiers' drawers, he led her to an open safe that held over 200 thousand crisp hundreds and twenties. "This is what I'm talking about," he said as he held one gun on the cashier and used the other hand to load the money.

YaYa shouted, "Sixty seconds!"

Jerusalem forced the cashier to the floor and stuffed as much money as he could into the bag.

"Forty-five seconds!" YaYa yelled, looking at his watch.

Jerusalem pointed the gun at the cashiers and the bank manager. "Get up." He directed them to walk around the counter. "Down. Now!" He demanded them to lie on the floor with the rest of the bank patrons.

Malachi walked the unarmed guard to the same location. "On the floor, motherfucka!"

"Fifteen seconds!" YaYa said.

Jerusalem passed the duffle bag to YaYa, who rushed out of the bank first and hopped into the SUV. He was unaware of the off duty undercover officer who happened to be in the area. The officer was entering the restaurant next door but stopped when he saw YaYa exit the bank.

Malachi exited next and climbed in the back of the SUV. They both kneeled down in the backseat.

Jerusalem, with his eyes still on the people on the floor, held his weapon in their direction, while backing up toward the door.

Pinky kept the SUV running, and was first to notice the plain-clothes officer. When he reached for his gun, she saw the sunlight reflect off the metal badge on his belt. "There go a motherfuckin' cop!" she yelled.

As Jerusalem backed up out the bank, the cop yelled, "Freeze, motherfucka, and slowly put down your weapon!"

Jerusalem turned and faced the cop with his weapon drawn. "No, you drop your weapon."

"Drop your fuckin' weapon now!" the cop demanded. "No, you drop your weapon!" Jerusalem replied calmly.

Pinky roared the engine to signal to Jerusalem that it was time to move out. Both the officer and Jerusalem turned their head toward the SUV. Malachi was in the backseat with the AK47 pointed at the off duty cop. Jerusalem eyed Pinky. Pinky looked at Jerusalem.

"Go!" Jerusalem said.

Pinky hesitated as sirens wailed in the distance. Water filled Pinky's eyes. She didn't want to leave him, but Jerusalem yelled out, "Bitch, did you hear what I said? Go!" Thinking Malachi was ready to fire at any second, YaYa pulled down Malachi's arm and said, "We got the money. No need for that. Jerusalem can take care of himself."

Malachi bit down on his bottom lip and reasoned with himself as YaYa told Pinky, "Drive, baby girl!"

Pinky smashed on the gas, dodging the bullets the officer fired toward the SUV. She sped off into oncoming traffic.

Jerusalem, using himself as a sacrifice to save his crew, set off running. A foot chase got underway. He dodged in and out between cars and turned a corner, hoping it would lead to an escape route to freedom. Two police cars sped out of nowhere and blocked his way. He turned and the plain- clothes officer was still coming fast behind him. He slipped in a shop and ran through the store knocking down items. Customers in the store screamed as he ran toward the back of the store looking for an exit door.

Pushing the door open, he ran down the alley away from the main street, while taking off his mask with one hand. He jumped over the wall as his heart beat out of control. Jerusalem hoped he'd lost the cops pursuing him. The moment he looked up, a group of officers were pointing their guns directly at him. He bent down and placed his weapon on the ground just in case a trigger happy cop was in their midst. Defeated, he lifted both hands in the air as the officers ordered him to the ground.

One of the officers rushed over to him and yelled, "Put your hands behind your back! You're under arrest!"

Tired and exhausted, Jerusalem did as ordered. The officer said, "You have the right to remain silent," as he picked Jerusalem up from the ground.

Jerusalem held his head back and closed his eyes as the officer continued to read him the Miranda rights.

The sound of the lock clicking brought Jerusalem back into present day—eight years after the bank heist.

Being in solitary confinement was a mental battle that Jerusalem Williams was determined to win. Dressed in just his boxers, he lay on the hard concrete floor of the jail cell with his hands locked behind his head staring up at the ceiling.

Like what you've read?
GO NOW TO WCLARKPUBLISHING.COM

ZAID ZA'HID

WAHIDA CLARK PRESENTS

SINCERELY, THE BOSS!

Sneak Peek

A Novel By
Wahida Clark & Amy Morford

This is a work of fiction. Names, characters, places, and incidents either are the product of the author's imagination or are used fictitiously, and any resemblance to actual persons, living or dead, business establishments, events, or locales is entirely coincidental.

Wahida Clark Presents Publishing, LLC
60 Evergreen Place
Suite 904
East Orange, New Jersey 07018
1 (866)-910-6920
www.wclarkpublishing.com

Copyright 2017 © by Amy Morford & Wahida Clark
All rights reserved. This book, or parts thereof, may not be reproduced in any form without permission.

ISBN 13-digit 978-1-944992-20-0
ISBN 10-digit 9781944992200
eBook ISBN 978-1-936649-11-2
Audio ISBN: 978-1-936649-08-02

Library of Congress Catalog Number
1. Urban, 2. Romance 3. Suspense 4. Mafia 5. Italian 6. New York City 7. Crime

Cover design and layout by Nuance Art, LLC
Book interior design by www.aCreativeNuance.com
Contributing Editors: Linda Wilson and R. Hamilton

Printed in United States

Prologue

*M*argo's phone rang, and she shrugged at Carol, as if to apologize for cutting her off. Secretly grateful to

have an excuse this time, she saw it was Abby again and wondered if this was an apology.

"Hello, sweetie," she started but Abigail cut her off. "Did you tell Dad that I wasn't in school?"

Margo could tell she was fuming. It seemed to be her daughter's normal state of emotion where Margo was concerned.

"I did," Margo confirmed. Abigail had been skipping school, and now she would blame her mother for whatever punishment David might dole out.

"I'm sorry, but I was worried about you." She had a million questions for Abby, none of which were going to get answered.

"I hate you!" Abigail screamed into the phone. "I hate you, and I wish you had just stayed in prison."

The line went dead. Margo let out a defeated sigh. She put the phone back in her bag and shrugged her shoulders at Carol.

"Kids!" she muttered to herself.

* * * *

Chapter 1

The alarm clock blared and Margo groaned as she felt for the off button. She glared at the time, a whole four hours of sleep and it was time to start all over again. After a year of working three jobs, sleep was what she longed for. The dreams, however, were a different story. She rolled out of bed, and her feet hit the floor. There was no point in letting herself wallow in her current situation. She might not be an optimist, but if the last seven years had taught her anything, it was that she was as tough as nails.

Margo wrapped the towel around herself after getting out of the shower. Damn, if there was one thing she missed about her house it was taking a long, hot bath in her whirlpool tub after a long day at the office. Living at the motel sucked, even though she didn't spend a lot of time here. The plumbing was old, and showers were either scalding hot or ice cold. This morning, she had chosen frigid over third-degree burns and she was covered in goose bumps. She scowled at her reflection. The worry lines had become permanent recently. She checked her face for any other disconcerting developments. At forty-three, Margo knew that she still turned heads, tall and curvy, with long, auburn hair, and intense, green eyes that were still a distraction for men.

She rolled her eyes; she was a distraction for all the *wrong* kind of men. How long had it been now? No, she didn't have time for fantasy. Reality occupied all of her time, and there was little chance that Prince Charming was going to walk into the diner this morning and, between coffee and the check, offer to whisk her away.

Margo checked her uniform and her backpack before heading out. She would return sometime around midnight, almost comatose, and she would barely get undressed before falling quickly to sleep again. At first when she started this routine, she had told herself that working long hours would help her stay sane. Lately, she wasn't so sure.

She didn't have time to second-guess herself, and that was a blessing. It was three hours into the breakfast shift and the diner was slammed. Margo had waited tables on and off when she was a teenager, but had gone to college so these kinds of menial jobs would be forever in the past. If she could give her own children one piece of advice now, it would be to never say never.

Margo knew it was after nine, but not before ten, because she saw Sal walk in. He strode through the diner like he owned the place, and for all Margo knew, he might have. His dark hair was slicked back neatly; the touches of gray made him look even more distinguished. His suit was impeccable as always. He was the only man that she'd seen in the year she worked here who wore cuff links. She had realized shortly after meeting him though that it wouldn't have mattered what he wore; he exuded a quiet power, and he knew it. The other customers were quiet when he passed by, and he took his usual seat. He always sat in her section.

Her cheeks flushed this morning when she picked up the coffeepot and headed in his direction. She blamed it on the fact that he flirted with her; sometimes she blamed it on the fact that she couldn't remember the last time she had sex, but Sal's attention lately had made her long for a little romance.

"Good morning, Sunshine. How's my favorite customer today?"

She smiled when she saw him. She couldn't help it; he was contagious and had that kind of effect on her with that twinkle of mischief in his eyes.

"Wonderful, Cookie, and how's my favorite waitress faring today?"

His voice was gruff, and if Margo was honest, she imagined him calling her "Cookie" during some intimate moments.

"Great, you want the usual?"

He gave her those smoldering eyes and the look that kept her simmering lately. "If I can't get anything else..."

Their banter went back to the day they met, but the flirtation had become more heated lately, and Margo went in the back and eyed him from the kitchen. She had heard the stories; according to Vinnie, the line cook with a lazy eye, Sal was powerful businessman with ties to the Mafia. From her past dealings with the criminal element, she believed it. He was definitely a man who knew how to get what he wanted.

When she returned with Sal's usual, a glass of orange juice, two eggs over easy, and a slice of dry wheat toast, he stopped her. "Hey, Cookie, you're a smart girl, let me ask you something."

"Sure, Sal, anything." It was a lie; Margo was very good at dodging answers.

"What are you doing working here?" He looked around to indicate that the diner might not be a career choice for someone with ambition and half a brain.

Margo shrugged. "I needed a job. Help wanted sign in the window, five-question interview, I fit in the uniform, and voilà. Hired on the spot. Do you need more coffee?"

She was quick to change the subject. No matter how attractive Sal might be and how much they flirted, there were certain subjects that were off-limits.

Her section filled up again quickly, and Margo must have been in the kitchen when Sal left. When she went back to his table and found it empty, she couldn't help but feel slightly disappointed. Sometimes conversation with Sal was just about the only thing that made her smile all day. Under his coffee cup, he had left his usual ten-dollar tip and she folded the money and slid it into her pocket.

At noon, it was time to change and get to her second job. Thankfully, the Laundromat didn't require that she wear a uniform as ridiculous as the getup she wore at the diner. It was far too low-cut and showed way too much leg. Margo had complained to Vinnie.

"I'm not making enough money here to flash cleavage." "Hey, think about how much less you'd make if you

didn't." He had winked at her with his good eye, and she knew that the case was closed.

Jeans and a tee shirt were all she needed for her second job and the peace and quiet there gave her time to work on her third job.

Margo walked the ten blocks from the diner to the Laundromat. This was her only real free time of the day, and she would stop, grab a quick bite from the deli and one more cup of coffee. She had to remind herself to eat lately; she had lost enough weight over the last few years, and there was no point in getting sick. The cell phone in her backpack rang as she was chewing. Margo swallowed quickly. She didn't get many calls.

"Hello?" she answered, clearing her throat. "Hello?" she repeated.

"Hey, Mom." It was Abigail, her daughter who should be in school right now. Margo immediately wondered why she was calling her, what was wrong.

"Honey, are you okay? Are you at school?" Her sweet little girl had grown up way too fast and Margo would never forgive herself for the role she had played in all of that.

"No, I stayed home today." Abigail had just turned fifteen and had started lying a lot lately. Rather than call her on it, Margo decided to let it slide. The kids hated her enough right now.

"I kind of need some money." There it was, the reason for the call.

"Sure, Abby." It was her daughter's nickname from a long time ago, and Margo didn't seem to be able to stop using it, even though her daughter hated it now.

"Sorry, Abigail," she corrected herself. "How much do you need?"

"Like five hundred would be good."

It seemed like an awful lot of cash for someone her age and Margo's pulse beat faster as she thought of the possibilities.

"Can you tell me what you need the money for, honey?"

She was trying so hard to make up for the past, but it didn't seem to matter what she did. Her words and actions were always wrong. She hoped Abigail didn't catch on to her try-hard sickly sweet voice.

Abigail sighed loudly, and Margo knew that she had lost.

Whatever the game was, she wasn't playing it right. "Never mind. Forget it. I'll just ask Dad."

Margo had to calm herself every time the kids brought up David, and she held her breath before answering.

"No, I can help—" she started, but her daughter had already hung up on her. Margo looked at the time and shoved the last two bites of her sandwich in her mouth, drained the coffee, and decided that she would walk and talk.

She pressed David's name on her phone and waited for him to pick up. Her ex-husband was probably having a leisurely lunch somewhere with clients, drinking espresso and enjoying an overpriced meal in a trendy place with five-star food and service. The good life. The life they used to have together. Margo missed it. It had all slipped away so quickly. Her call went to voice mail and Margo wanted to scream. Of course he would screen his calls, especially hers. "Hey, asshole," she started her message, "what the fuck does my daughter need five hundred dollars for? Do you even know what our children are doing all day? Do you know that Abigail isn't in school right now? Get your worthless ass home and check on the kids, damn it!"

She pressed end call and stood outside the Laundromat for a moment. Her heart was pounding, and her blood seemed to boil in her veins. No matter what she did, it wasn't enough for Abigail and Thomas, and it seemed like David could do no wrong. Margo had lost them long ago and sometimes she felt like it would have been kinder if she had simply died instead of having her heart broken again and again.

She went inside and waved at Carol, the heavyset woman who worked the mornings.

"You're not going to believe what happened," Carol began.

She always wanted to give Margo the blow-by-blow account of the people that had been in, the minutia of what had happened. Margo had learned long ago to just set up her laptop in the back and start typing. Carol seemed to have less to say to the back of her head.

"Uh-huh," Margo said. She barely pretended to be interested but that was enough for Carol. She was oblivious to whether Margo listened or not.

She waved good-bye as her coworker walked out the door.

It was time to start her third job.

Margo had been writing as a freelancer over the last year, and it was the most lucrative job that she could find. In college, she always had her assignments written well ahead of their due dates. Writing had always come easy to her; she had a knack for it. Now she wrote term papers for spoiled college kids who would pass off her work as their own, that and anything else people wanted to pay her for. How could she blame people for a little plagiarism when she was a convicted felon?

Like what you've read?
VISIT THE FOLLOWING LINK TO ORDER NOW
http://amzn.to/2up0B5Z

WAHIDA CLARK PRESENTS

The Pink Panther Clique:

Sneak Peek

By
Aisha Hall, Sunshine Smith-Williams,
Jamila T. Davis with Wahida Clark

This is a work of fiction. Names, characters, places, and incidents either are the product of the author's imagination or are used fictitiously, and any resemblance to actual persons, living or dead, business establishments, events, or locales are entirely coincidental.

Wahida Clark Presents Publishing
60 Evergreen Place
Suite 904A
East Orange, New Jersey 07018
1(866)-910-6920
www.wclarkpublishing.com

Copyright 2017 © by Aisha Hall, Sunshine Smith-Williams, Jamila T. Davis with Wahida Clark

All rights reserved. This book, or parts thereof, may not be reproduced in any form without permission.

Library of Congress Cataloging-In-Publication Data:
Aisha Hall, Sunshine Smith-Williams, Jamila T. Davis
Pink Panther Clique Preview

ISBN 13-digit 978-1936649556 (paperback)
ISBN 13-digit 978-1936649730 (ebook)
ISBN 13-digit: 978-1936649709 (Hardback)
LCCN: 2017904236

1. New York, NY - 2. Money Laundering 3. Hip Hop- 4. African American-Fiction- 5. Music Industry- 6. Federal Prisoners-

Cover design and layout by Nuance Art, LLC
Book design by NuanceArt@aCreativeNuance.com
Edited by Linda Wilson
Proofreader Alanna Boutin
Printed in USA

Prologue

She swallowed a basketball. Her big, pregnant belly protruded, giving off that impression.

"There's no way she should *still* be pregnant. She looks like she's about to drop that load any day now," Sun-Solé, a short, voluptuous, caramel-toned woman with long, straight hair said.

"Shhh. Girl, they're going to hear us. Just keep mopping," Eshe warned. She was a tall, chinky-eyed, brown-skinned girl with a strong New York swagger.

"I can't believe y'all got me down here," Milla said. She was a bright-eyed, almond-toned diva who, even in prison, kept her clothes crisp and her makeup on fleek.

The three women watched from a distance as the pregnant girl wobbled to her seat in the visiting room. They pretended to be cleaning, but they were there for a completely different reason. Sun-Solé was the main one who insisted they volunteer as prison orderlies today, because she could smell drama in the air.

"I'm telling y'all," Sun-Solé said, "I heard Prego on the phone. Baby daddy is coming today. Shit's gonna hit the fan, word to mutha."

Milla rolled her eyes at Sun-Solé. She found it funny to see her prison sister with a mop in her hand because, on the contrary, Sun-Solé was a grown-ass princess. Milla knew how her girl truly lived. Maids and assistants did everything at her home, and she never lifted a finger. Sun-Solé's domestic act had Milla chuckling to herself. Those who only knew her in prison would assume Sun-Solé was a regular Suzy Homemaker who took every cleaning job the prison offered. Anything to get her off the cell block and onto Gossip Street. Sun-Solé cleaned every place from the warden's office to the guards' locker room. Then she'd report all that was going on in the prison to Eshe and Milla. She even knew what was happening in the men's facility. But that was an entirely different story.

Sun-Solé, Eshe, and Milla's eyes were like three sharp surveillance cameras, recording every moment, each of them looking on for various reasons. Sun-Solé was the entertainer. She thought everything was a movie, but instead of it being on the big-screen, she watched things play out in real time. Life was one big reality show to her. She took in the whole scene of

Prego with her baby daddy and got high from the action of it all.

Milla watched because she wanted to write about every single injustice that was done to each woman in the prison system. She wanted to tear it down, brick by brick, one story at a time, and end mass incarceration once and for all. She hated the American so-called criminal justice system with a passion because it destroyed families. Specifically, women.

Eshe was extremely unconventional. The female corporate thug, a walking almanac who could probably tell you what the weather was like on any given day in the sixth century. The pragmatic one of the group, Eshe moved when driven by logic only and tried to intervene in situations where she could be of help by adding her opinion. Sometimes, it worked; other times, she had to get a bit ratchet and remind chicks where she was from. Eshe got along with everyone, for the most part, but would buck on the guards at any moment.

All of the ladies were from New York, and they moved with a different swag. They observed Prego on the DL, to see how she would get out of the situation. Prego was just a nickname for the pregnant girl whom they'd been observing. Prego's boyfriend stared her down with a confused look.

"This doesn't feel right. You denied my visits all this time. This shouldn't be the first time I'm seeing you.

You won't call me. I'm starting to lose my mind. And look at you; you're as big as a house. This doesn't add up. How can you possibly still be pregnant?"

"You don't understand."

"You've been locked up for ten months and two weeks. You found out you were pregnant before you got here. What the hell is going on? I mean, you need to see a specialist— something! You're going to explode. This shit ain't normal," Prego's boyfriend said.

"There's something I need to tell you." Prego did not look at her man. She stared at the floor as if looking for a quick escape. But there was no escaping reality. At least, not for the ladies in Danbury Federal Prison.

"Well, what is it, baby? It's bad enough you're in here carrying my first child. Is there some type of medical condition I need to know about?" he asked, raising his hands and shaking his head. His perplexed expression caused all three spies to immediately label him as stupid. It didn't matter that he was an attorney. He was a plain ol' dumb ass.

"Visitation is over!" the officer yelled out. "Emergency lockdown. I repeat, visitation is over."

"Awww, shit," one of the spies whispered. "Damn. It's about to go down. Lieutenant Longwood is walking toward them. Look, girl!" Sun-Solé was so excited to see what was about to unfold. Milla was ready to go, and Eshe was in protection mode.

Lieutenant Longwood stepped in front of Prego and her man. "Do you all not hear well? Visitation is over."

"As far as I know, according to policy, visits trump all other prison matters. I'm an attorney. I'm seeing my pregnant fiancée for the first time in months. Can you just give us a minute?" Prego still looked at the floor.

"I don't care what *you* do, but her . . . *She* is going back to her unit, now!" Then he did the unthinkable: he grabbed Prego by her arm and lifted her from her seat. Then he whispered something in her ear. A tear fell from her eye.

"Hey, don't put your hands on her like that. Man, are you crazy?" Prego's baby daddy said. Lieutenant Longwood released her arm and folded his own arms across his chest.

"You got *one* minute!"

"Baby, does this man do this often? I am going to file a complaint," he said in a low tone.

"Don't bother. I'm stuck here. They do what they want." "Time's up!" Longwood stated.

"Can I at least give her a kiss? Damn!"

"Hell, no!" he said. "As a matter of fact, Inmate Gaines, don't you have something to tell this clown?"

"Clown? Man, what the fuck is your issue?"

"Not now, Longwood. I'll tell him next time," Prego said. "Next time? There won't be a next time. You need to let him know, or I will. Today is my last day here, so it needs to

be done." She nodded and another tear fell from her eye. "Okay, I'm gonna just come out and say it."

"Say what?" Baby Daddy asked.

"I'm with Lieutenant Longwood. This is his baby, not yours." Milla, Eshe, and Sun-Solé's mouths dropped open.

"This shit ain't right!" Eshe whispered.

"Well, what the hell are we supposed to do?" Milla added. "Nothing. What can we do?" Sun-Solé said. By this time, none of them were even pretending to clean. They were just watching. The visiting room was damn near empty, so there

was nobody else around to see what was going down.

It was only for a second that they'd looked at each other to speak, but a second was all it took for chaos to break out. By the time they looked back at the love triangle, Baby Daddy was swinging at Lieutenant Longwood. He snuffed the homie.

Crack!

Longwood's jaw fractured. At least that's what it sounded like. Longwood removed his flashlight and caught Baby Daddy in the head. He fell backward. An alarm sounded, and correction officers were every-damn-where. They were pulling Longwood off of Baby

Daddy, and another group had pushed the spies to the corner.

Then suddenly there was a piercing cry. "My stomach!" Prego called out. "Oh God! I think my water broke!" The fight was broken up, and medical workers were paged. Milla, Eshe, and Sun-Solé broke through the human barricade of guards who were guarding them in the corner and ran to Prego.

"It's going to be all right," Eshe said, sitting Prego onto the floor.

"No, it's not," she whispered. "This baby ain't neither one of theirs!"

"What! Who's the father?" Eshe asked.

More guards arrived in the visiting room, and they ordered the three spies to get up against the wall so they could be cuffed and taken back to their unit. Sun-Solé was ear hustling. Her hearing was on high alert like a bunny's ears. But nobody heard anything because there was too much noise and chaos. There was blood everywhere from both Lieutenant Longwood and Baby Daddy. Eshe turned around one last time to look at Prego, and she quickly mouthed one name to her. A name they all knew.

Nahhhhh. It can't be! The scandal was deeper than anyone could have ever imagined, and shit was about to hit the fan!

* * * *

Chapter 1

Milla

♫ *You the only one I love (uh-huh)/The only man I know that I can trust (yup)/And if I ever should need you, I know you'll come (yeah) ready to kill with a smoking gun (with a smoking gun).* ♫

I sang passionately to Jadakiss's song "Smoking Gun." The words made me think about love and how it used to feel. But at this very moment, the most important thing on my mind was money. I put L. Boogie, Jill Scott, and Adele on rotation to keep me in my zone. Until my office phone rang and interrupted me. After five rings, I picked up. My boss's extension showed on the display in big, black digital numbers.

"Yes, Mr. Darding," I answered.

"Ms. Davison, I need to see you in my office . . . pronto!" "Sure thing." I hung up and sat there awhile.

Although he was my boss, I wasn't the type of employee who asked how high when a higher-up told me to jump. After I was good and ready, I turned my music off and got into professional mode. Professional mode was something that came natural to me, but so did my street persona.

By the way, my name is Jamila Davison, but I go by the name of Milla. I work for Standard American Bank, also known as SAB, one of the largest banks in the country. Currently, I'm a loan agent, and I've got the best track record in our district. I close millions of dollars' worth of loans every single month, and my numbers are steadily increasing. In other words, I'm a beast when it comes to finance. But once I left the office and got into the comfort of my whip, I opened my ashtray, lit up some bud, and blasted Jadakiss. I knew how to turn it on and off. It was a survival mechanism that I'd learned over the years while growing up in Queens. I am who I am, a true black woman who loves her culture. I could pick up a mic and spit a verse with the dudes I grew up with, or I could pick up a mic and sell our bank's latest loan products to a crowd of investors. Because I was equipped with a skill set that allowed me to indulge in the best of both worlds, I was a true chameleon. I grew up not missing a beat in the streets, but also staying on top of my schooling. I was sure my persona would take me far, and I would soon find out just how far once I walked into Mr. Darding's office.

"Ms. Davison. How are you?" he said upon me entering. "I'm fine. How about you, sir?" I replied, shaking his

hand.

"Good, good. Have a seat." I sat my well-rounded booty in the comfort of the black leather chair in front of his desk. He adjusted his seat so he could keep an eye on my legs. And like a salivating dog, he licked his lips as I crossed one leg over the other. *Men. So damn predictable.* It took everything in me to not burst out laughing. Darding was about fifty-five years old, partially bald, with an oversized gut. I didn't give a damn how much money he had; I would never bounce up and down on his lap. Never. Ugh! But still, I smiled, anxious to know what he wanted from me.

"Is everything all right? I see that you wanted me to come here right away. I can't say I'm not nervous. Being called into the principal's office is not always a good thing." He laughed.

"Milla. May I call you Milla?"

"Sure. I prefer it actually. We're all family here at SAB." I threw on the charm, but I wished he would get to the damn point.

"Well, you're here because today is a very special day for you. There's something we noticed about you."

I cleared my throat. "Like what?"

"Most of the clients whom you've been giving loans to are rappers and other famous African Americans. Also, you've been bringing in other individuals who are . . . ummm, let's just say, not the *typical* clients we see come into our bank. Or any bank for that matter." He chuckled at his own joke. I did not. Then I started to think about this impromptu meeting . .. *Awww, shit. If he's going to fire me, he needs to just get to it and stop horsing around. I put a lot of blood, sweat, and tears into this bank. Hell, I brought in new business however I could. So if they're trying to get rid of me, I got a few choice words for his ass!*

So here is the raw truth about how I played the banking game: I just happened to see an opportunity with these celebrities and wanted to help them while helping myself. I had to pull teeth sometimes to get them approved for loans. I even had to tell little white lies sometimes because a lot of them didn't have tax returns or had cash businesses. But what I did was still good. Helping guys with new record deals get their first Bentley, Maybach, Rolls-Royce, or Lamborghini. Taking dope boys from the projects to gated communities. So what, I made up pay stubs. They paid their bills, and that was all that mattered. I was making the bank lots of money because all my people paid their loans back. They better had, or else they would have to deal with me personally. I figured I would sell myself before he gave me the bad news. You know, try to save face.

"I just spoke with Jadakiss. He's a famous rapper right here in New York, and he was approved for a $2 million mortgage not too long ago. I got him to put a million down, so he's well invested. I can tell you, I know him personally, and he will not only pay, but pay early. And Zab Judah, five- time champion boxer, he just paid off a $3.5 million loan that I worked very hard to get for him. I know my methods were a little nontraditional, but my goal is to make this bank #1 in the world. The world, sir. No other bank could do it, but I got it done. If there is something wrong with the—" He interrupted me.

"No, there is nothing wrong. Actually, we think what you're doing is great. You're bringing in some unusual characters, yes, and it's making the bank a lot of money. There is some good news that recently came down the pipeline." He leaned in closer from his side of the desk. "We want to promote you. We want you to bring more of your, uh, your people into our establishment. It's a win-win situation for all of us." He got up and closed his office door, then sat back down and talked in a hushed tone.

"I know a lot of these rapper characters don't have good credit, Milla. We also noticed you seem to know a lot of . .."—now he went into an all-out whisper—"drug dealers and street guys. But they still have plenty of money, and we can still sell houses to these people. We just need you and your wit to help continue to bridge that gap. We'll give you whatever you need. There is just one condition."

"Okay . . . and what's that?" His breath stank of the rotten bullshit that was about to fly out of his mouth any second. *Here it comes.*

"Well, all of these types of loans need to start with 14 percent interest."

"Fourteen percent?" I repeated, shocked. I looked at him as if he'd passed me the whip and asked me to beat his slaves for him. He'd lost his mind. My stare lingered. *He can't be serious. That amount is outrageous!* I was about to get up and walk out, but I pondered his offer briefly. Yeah, he thought he was getting over by exploiting my people, giving them high interest loans that any knowledgeable person would never pay. However, I saw an opportunity to help a lot of people, and my brain had already started churning out a plan to get around that interest rate crap. I could work my magic once I got an opportunity to get creative. And it sounded like he was giving me that power.

"What exactly would the position be?"

"Special accounts manager."

"And the meaning of *special*?" I asked, raising a freshly waxed eyebrow.

"Well, we'll leave that to you. We can get creative. But, of course, we want the bank to be known for bridging the gap and giving minorities opportunities that no other bank has done. And the best part of it is: we'll give you your own team with underwriting power to approve loans up to $5 million! We've got about $500 million to lend. Who knows, you can be the Oprah Winfrey savior for your people. Think about what you can do. Not just for yourself, but for your community." Never in America does a bank suddenly tell a black person they have access to so much money, to give to more black folks. *Something is off with this. This is corporate America, and we aren't welcome here.*

"Of course, I'll accept. I love it! Thank you so much for the opportunity, Mr. Darding." We shook on it. My name was already ringing bells. I surely didn't want to sound off any alarms. If I felt that he was up to something crazy, I would back out. But I'd wait until that happened, if ever.

I exited the bank, jumped in my Benz, and celebrated with a fat-ass blunt. Yeah, Milla Winfrey had a crazy ring to it! But I also found out that if something sounded too good to be true . . . it usually was!

Like what you've read?
GO NOW TO
WCLARKPUBLISHING.COM

WAHIDA CLARK PRESENTS

PRETTY BOY HUSTLERZ

Part 1

VICTOR L. MARTIN

This is a work of fiction. Names, characters, places, and incidents either are the product of the author's imagination or are used fictitiously, and any resemblance to actual persons, living or dead, business establishments, events, or locales are entirely coincidental.

Wahida Clark Presents Publishing
60 Evergreen Place
Suite 904A
East Orange, New Jersey 07018
1(866)-910-6920
www.wclarkpublishing.com

Copyright 2017 © by Victor L. Martin
All rights reserved. This book, or parts thereof, may not be reproduced in any form without permission.

Library of Congress Cataloging-In-Publication Data:
Victor L. Martin
Pretty Boy Hustlerz

ISBN 13-digit 978-1-944992-76-7 (paper)
ISBN 10-digit 9871944992767 (paper)
LCCN: 2017904232

1. North Carolina- 3. Drug Trafficking- 4. African American-Fiction- 5. Urban Fiction- 6. Prison Life

Cover design and layout by Nuance Art, LLC
Art direction layout: www.artdiggs.com

Printed in USA

ALSO BY VICTOR L. MARTIN

Pretty Boy Hustlerz 1 & 2
Nude Awakening II: Still Nude
Nude Awakening
The Game of Deception

Anthologies
What's Really Hood?
(with Wahida Clark, Bonta, Shawn "Jihad" Trump, and LaShonda Teague)
Even Sinners Still Have Souls
(with Darrell King, Tysha, and Michel Moore)

CHAPTER ONE

Selma, North Carolina
June 11th, Tuesday
Present Time

"I can't keep living like this, Lorenzo!" Shayla Graham shouted with tears filling her eyes. She wiped them and stared at her boyfriend from across the bedroom.

"Do you know what I got in the mail today? More bills! Overdue bills that you promised to help me with. Every month you have a new excuse with your half of the bills. The rent is behind. My car is about to be repossessed. And nearly every damn night I have to feed our son some noodles!"

"You act like I don't have no bills of my own!" Lorenzo fired back.

"What bills! How the hell you gonna convince me that you need some chrome rims on your cars?" She yelled. "We're about to be homeless! And all you do is front like shit is sweet when you know our shit is fucked up. You can't be like, Travis and rip and run the streets and blow money. What you need to do is maintain your home like a real man is supposed to!"

"Ain't trying to be like Travis!" Lorenzo shoved his arm through the ironed sleeves of his uniform.

"I can't tell!" Shayla glared at Lorenzo. "Ever since you got that job at the prison you've been trying to do what Travis do. FYI Travis doesn't have the responsibilities that you have. You have a son Lorenzo. We're about to lose everything baby. If I have to move back to Smithfield with my mom, where will you go? What? Back up to Michigan with your family."

"I'm doing the best I can, Shayla! I can't give you what I don't have."

"Something has to change. And it has to be now. Every damn day I'm having to beg for overtime at Walmart and nine times out of ten I never get it. I can't keep giving you gas money when my own damn tank stays on empty."

"It's not like I'm not trying, Shayla." He turned to face her. "I hate being broke all the time and living from check to check."

Shayla flopped down on the foot of the bed with her chin down. "This is driving me crazy! Why is this happening to me? It's the same problems every month," she murmured. "If I lose this home, I don't know what will become of us, Lorenzo."

"Shayla," Lorenzo called out. "What?" She looked up.

"Baby, I know times are hard. But you have to believe in me.

Have some faith in me."

"Believing in you and having faith in you isn't going to keep a roof over our heads. I swear I'm trying to stick this one out with you." Shayla softened her tone.

"Times get hard and you wanna break up!" "I didn't say that," she replied.

"So, what was that shit about you not knowing what will become of us!"

Her eyes began to pool with fresh tears. She crossed her arms and looked down at the floor, slightly rocking back and forth. *Maybe I would be better off by myself. Just my son and I. But God, I love Lorenzo*, she thought with a hurting heart.

"Talk to me, Shayla. Where all this breaking up bullshit coming from? Over some fucking bills?"

"It's not just some fucking bills!" she snapped. "It's us, Lorenzo! Our life. Our present and our future. But you know what?" she shot to her feet and glared at him. "I'm willing to do whatever to keep this place our home! If I have to—" she paused to wipe her tears. "I'll go to Wilson and work out at"

"No the fuck you ain't!" Lorenzo butted in. "That bullshit ain't even up for discussing! You can dead that idea and I mean it, Shayla!"

"But."

"No! I meant what I said, Shayla. I'll figure something out, okay."

Shayla bit her tongue on the job opportunity in Wilson. Beefing with Lorenzo wasn't helping her issue. She no longer cared what he wanted to discuss or not. Shayla had a fix to ease the issue of her bills, and at this point, she felt cornered into doing it behind Lorenzo's back.

***

Lorenzo Watson arrived at Maury Correctional Institution with his troubles still pressing. The only good thing so far was being posted in the control booth from 6 p. m. to 10 p. m. Since lockdown was called at 11:00 p. m., it would only be one hour of dealing with the worrisome ass inmates. From his seat in the booth he could see all three blocks, A, B, and C. Each block held forty-eight grown men, but in Watson's view, it was nothing but a fucking daycare center. For the next twelve hours, his goal was to sit on his ass and do next to nothing. He never gave the inmates a hard time and he was known to turn a blind eye on a number of wrong doings. As long as they weren't trying to kill each other or escape, Watson stayed in his lane. All he wanted was his two checks a month and that was it. Around 9:00 p.m., operations made the announcement to lockdown for count. As always it was ignored by 90% of the inmates. They wouldn't move from the card table or TV's until an officer came inside the block. Watson could've been an ass by turning the TV's off but that wasn't his temper. The three floor officers and the sergeant started with C block to lockdown. For the next few minutes, Watson had to respond to his radio and pop the cells open for each inmate to lockdown. The task was the norm to Watson, dull and boring to be honest. When all of the dorms were cleared he scanned the control board to make sure all of the cell doors were secured.

"All cell doors are secured for A, B, and C dorms," Watson said over the radio.

"Ten-four," Sergeant Karen Parker replied.

Watson reached for his soda when the phone rung inside the booth. "North side control," he answered.

"What's up, Watson? You in the booth again tonight?" Officer Lisa Hart asked.

"Yeah and I hope to stay up here. What's up with you down there?"

"Just wrote up one of these nasty ass clowns down here jacking off on me in the shower! Wrote his natural black ass right on up! I hate that nasty shit!"

Watson laughed, "Who was it?"

"Um…Charles Pender in E-block. Seriously, not that I would fuck an inmate but damn, what happened to all these men with the solid talk game? First moment these fools see a woman in the booth they fly up to the shower and leave the curtain wide the fuck open. I see enough dick at home. Shit burns me the fuck up!" Hart griped.

"What time you gonna take your break?" Watson asked after Hart finished venting.

"Uh… around midnight. Why? What's up?"

"Just asking. Oh, where Dixon at?"

"Mr. Travis Dixon is in F-block locking the kids down which is taking forever because he's too laid back."

"Tell 'im to come holler at me after count."

"Boy, please. Y'all two are like brothers. You already know his ass will be down there to see you. But I'll relay the message anyway."

"Okay, thanks."

"Oh, and guess who got walked out yesterday on the other shift?"

"Who?"

"Williamson up on green unit."

"Word! Talking 'bout the white girl with black hair?"

"Yep. Her dumpy ass got caught in the storage room with

the canteen man."

"Damn! How she get caught up?"

"From the inmate running his fucking mouth! He told one too many of his homeboys and one of 'em dropped a letter on his ass. She also was dumb enough to send dude some nude pics to his cell phone that was found in his cell. I tell ya, a man in prison will fuck any woman breathing. Now I know I can stand to lose a few pounds myself…but ole girl was obese!" Officer Hart rambled.

"Will she be charged?"

"I doubt it but her fat ass is out of a job that's for damn sure. I guess she couldn't handle all the attention she got in here and fell for the first line of game thrown in her direction. I ain't listening to none of the bullshit these fools in here trying to spit. Fuck that. Motherfuckers can't pay my rent or car note, ain't talking 'bout shit, and that's just keeping it real!"

"True." Watson nodded.

"Well lemme get my ass off this phone so I can call my girl over on red unit."

"Thanks, Hart and I mean that." *It's because we got an empty refrigerator.* Watson thought.

Watson ended the call with Hart aka Miss Gossip Queen. She was cool and easy to deal with and had trained Watson when he first started working. She was in her mid-forties, married with two kids and having an affair with Dixon. Plus she favored Oprah Winfrey.

At 9:23 p. m., Watson wrote in the logbook that the count was cleared. The control board lit up as each inmate pressed their call button for their cell door to be popped. It was an easy task, pressing a button beside each blinking red light. It took Watson under two minutes to let everyone out. Watching the monitor he saw the feminine guy in B-block sliding inside another man's cell. Up on the top tier, an inmate gestured for the shower to be turned on. Watson flipped the switch for all the showers, then leaned back in the chair. Nothing hard at all about his job. Thinking of his troubles he realized he still had a better life than the 144 inmates in the three blocks. Any one of them would trade places to be free without a second thought. Watson had to come up with a plan to earn more money to keep his life together.

His pride took a beating by Shayla's words but all she had spoken was the truth. He had a family to support and was worried if he could man up to it. His first line of thinking centered around pulling overtime. It would force him to deal with that dumb ass, straight-laced sergeant on B-rotation. Slumped in the chair he tried to keep it together when Dixon entered the booth at 9:50 p.m.

Dixon and Watson were indeed the best of friends. Dixon had been a CO at MCI for five years and by all accounts, he loved his job. Both were on their pretty boy swag. At the age of twenty-four, Watson's dark tone and forever fresh haircut placed him in favor of Trey Songz. Travis, two years older, had a much lighter tone from his mixed race genes, set in likeness to Drake. Both stood at six feet even with an average build that suited their frames.

"Damn I'm tired," Dixon flopped down on a gray plastic chair beside Watson. He wore his state-issued Department of Public Safety cap like a fitted over his waves.

"I don't see how 'cause you ain't done shit." Watson joked. "This unit couldn't run without me and you know it." "Yeah right."

"You just mad because I get to do my own thang up in here," Dixon grinned.

"Hell, you fucking Hart so that shouldn't be a big ass surprise."

"Whoa bruh," Dixon smiled. "Check it, I don't *fuck* Hart... I only have sex with 'er so get it right. Now with my jump off, I fucks her sweet ass every chance I get and the pussy is hella good. For real, Asian girls do it better."

"That's TMI for me." Watson laughed. "I just hope you don't get caught up in your ways."

"Man, fuck them hoes. Why were you looking all spaced out in line up? Something wrong?"

Watson sighed. If there was anyone he could rap with and keep it 100, it was Dixon. "I might need to put in for some overtime to make ends meet. Bills are piling up on me, bruh."

"Shayla still working?" Dixon wondered. *With her fine ass!* Dixon secretly lusted.

"Yeah. But her checks ain't what they used to be," Watson complained.

"I'm glad I don't have any kids. Word up, I keep my shit covered all the time. But anyway how much are you behind with your bills?" Dixon asked as he removed his cap.

Watson scratched his chin. "'Round like five thousand." "Man, working on B-rotation is gonna stress you the fuck out. Sergeant Miles ain't worth shit," Dixon stated.

"Ain't got no other choice, bruh. I got a family to support so all that other shit, I'll just have to deal with it and do me."

Dixon figured Watson's issues were bad since he had lent him a few dollars for lunch last week. "Man, if you do that they might move you to B-rotation since they are already short of staff." *Yeah. Get moved to B-rotation so I can dip over on the low to Shayla. Man, I'd love to see that tight little ass in a thong!*

"It don't matter yo. I got no other choice. I figure I can swing a couple of overtime shifts to get over this ditch 'til I get back on my feet. I'ma talk to Parker on my break and see what's up."

"Don't do it," Dixon shook his head. *Yeah, do it. Shayla don't need your broke ass anyway.*

"What! Are you listening, bruh? Shit is fucking crazy at home and my money is looking funny so–"

"Bruh, you have another choice." *Shit! I might as well help him out.*

"Oh yeah? Where?" Watson looked all around the booth then threw his arms up in the air.

"Can I trust you?" Dixon lowered his voice with a serious expression.

Watson crossed his arms. "What do you think? And how does that matter about the fact of me needing money?"

"Why do you think I like this job so much?"

Watson shrugged. "Is it these low self-esteem women you be chasing?"

"Fuck no!" Dixon stood. "Bruh, I'ma put you up on game cause I fucks with you. No bullshit… I trap this money every day up in this bitch."

Watson frowned. "You ain't on the block no more, bruh, and I'm talking about the streets. In a few eyes… we the fucking police… the man. Listen to what the inmates yell when we make rounds in the blocks. 'Block is hot. Man down.' So how are you trapping?"

Dixon's pride pushed him to prove Watson wrong. Once his pride was mixed with his ego it was a wrap. "How you think guys up in here be failing those drug tests and shit?"

"What does it have to do with me because I really don't care?"

"It can have a lot to do with you if you're tired of being short on money. Listen, I told you I was renting them rims on my Lac right? Well, I paid for them the same day with cash."

Watson shifted in his chair, not understanding why Dixon had lied. "Those Rucci rims cost three stacks–"

"And I paid cash." Dixon cut in.

"Okay, you don't have bills like I do so you can–"

"That ain't the point, bruh. When I said I'm trapping, that's what I mean. This job is a gold mine and you don't even see it. When they took tobacco out of prison it was a blessing."

"How?" Watson was curious.

Dixon sat back down. "So I can trust you?"

Watson was hooked on how Dixon made money behind bars. The lure of easing the weight of his money issues was too tempting to let pass. If Dixon could spent $3,000 for a set of rims, then Watson wanted to do the same. "Yeah you can trust me. Now tell me what you got baking."

This is a work of fiction. Names, characters, places, and incidents either are the product of the author's imagination or are used fictitiously, and any resemblance to actual persons, living or dead, business establishments, events, or locales is entirely coincidental.

Wahida Clark Presents Publishing, LLC
60 Evergreen Place
Suite 904
East Orange, New Jersey 07018
1(866)910-6920
www.WClarkPublishing.com

Copyright 2011 © by Victor L. Martin
All rights reserved. This book, or parts thereof, may not be reproduced in any form without permission.

Nude Awakening
ISBN 13-digit 978-0-975964-62-0 (Paperback)
ISBN 10-digit 0-9759646-2-3
ISBN 13-digit 978-1-944992-12-5 (Hardback)
ISBN 10-digit 1-9449921-2-X
ISBN 13-digit 978-1-936649-91-4 (Ebook)
Library of Congress Catalog Number 2011905654

1. Urban, Porn, South Beach, Miami, Florida, African---American, Street Lit – Fiction

Cover design and layout by Oddball Design
Book interior design by Nuance Art.*.
www.DesignsByNuance.com
Contributing Editors: Linda Wilson, Maxine Thompson and Rosalind Hamilton

Printed in United States

Prologue
Summer of 1996 - Miami, Florida

Not guilty! Not guilty! Not guilty!

Eighteen-year-old Trevon Harrison could still hear those unjust words ringing in his anger-clouded mind. Six days ago, he had sat in the courtroom and watched the man accused of raping his thirteen-year-old sister await his verdict. Trevon sat with his mother as the ruthless attorney cross-examined his sister Angie to the point of tears. Because of his mother's presence, Trevon held his peace. The entire trial was bullshit. He doubted not a word of what happened when Angie stormed into his bedroom with tears in her eyes.

Trevon hated how the defense attorney weakened Angie's testimony. Since Angie's teacher had given her a failing grade, the attorney claimed her testimony was false. A simple act of revenge. There was no physical evidence to back up Angie. Trevon's testimony, a retelling of his sister's version of events was helpless.

It was so fresh in his young mind when the judge gave the verdict. The sick, child-molesting teacher had sunk back in his chair with a smile of relief on his pale face. Angie and his mother slipped out of the courtroom in tears. Trevon remained seated as a taste of detest filled him fully. There was no *justice* here. None. The only *justice* that made any sense was the type Trevon was willing to give. As the days turned over, he watched Angie turn into a quiet soul. His mother felt it was best to move them away.

Four days after the trial, Trevon heard the teacher on a local radio station speaking on the horror and pain of being falsely accused. Trevon listened to every lying word as his mother and sister packed up for the move to North Carolina. The radio host had asked the teacher how he felt toward Angie.

"I forgive her. She's just a troubled child. But in the end. One day she'll have to answer to a higher calling for telling that lie on me."

Trevon called Angie into his room with fresh tears filling his eyes. He did not question if she had told him the truth. To do so would have crushed whatever glimmer of life she still kept inside. He told her he knew the man had raped her and that she was not the young, scheming, lying, revengeful girl the attorney labeled her.

"The judge said he ain't guilty." Angie sobbed on his shoulder.

Trevon, at eighteen, had too much to shoulder. He would never be at peace without *justice*. No justice . . . no peace.

"Promise me you'll finish school when you get to North Carolina." Angie nodded, too deep in her sorrow to understand that Trevon was not planning on making the trip.

"I love you, lil sis."

Trevon stood hidden in the bushes under the sweltering sun. In his hand he held a slightly rusted snub–nosed .38 that was prone to misfire. Mr. Falston, Angie's English Lit teacher was standing in his manicured front yard peacefully watering the lawn. His back was toward Trevon. A green Acura Legend was parked in the driveway with a small poodle sitting under the front bumper cooling off. The front door of the house Mr. Falston shared with his wife was open. Music from a radio flowed out of the house. Trevon thought about the sick things Mr. Falston had done to his sister. No *justice* . . . no peace. Closing his eyes, Trevon mumbled a short prayer. He wanted the best for his mom and sister. Though he felt he was doing the right thing, he had yet to learn the danger of acting on anger. Opening his eyes, he saw Mr. Falston moving down a row of yellow and blue flowers with the water hose. The day was perfect. One of peace and quiet.

The poodle raised its head when Trevon emerged from the bushes. Its tail began to wag. Mr. Falston paused to wipe a coat of sweat off his forehead. He was almost done with his yard work. He was doing his best to put the trial behind him. At forty-four years old, he had to be more careful with his pickings of young girls. Angie was not the first underaged girl he had molested at school, nor would she be his last. He would learn from his mistakes with Angie. In his thinking, he felt he had not taken his time with her. When his poodle yelped, he turned around.

"What's the fuss, Missy?" Mr. Falston dropped the water hose when he spotted Trevon standing two feet away with Missy jumping and yelping around his legs wanting to play.

"You-you shouldn't be here." Mr. Falston took a step backward, quickly looking around for help. "I'm going to call the police if you don't leave . . ." His words ran into a gate when Trevon raised the .38.

Trevon held his aim true and dead center of Mr. Falston's chest. The poodle circled his feet. "Why did you do those things to Angie?"

Mr. Falston took another step backward, crushing the flowers. "You're . . . you're—her brother. Look. Just put the gun down. I know you're upset, so—"

"You don't know how I fucking feel!" Trevon's voice was loud and sharp. The poodle froze, tilted its head, then scampered off back toward the car.

"Son . . . please listen—"

"Ain't your damn son! The only father I knew . . ." Trevon blinked and raised his free hand to steady the pistol. "You said my sister would have to answer to a higher calling, right!"

"I—please put the gun down."

Trevon's head snapped to the left. A police siren. Across the street he saw a curtain falling back in place. Trevon kept the .38 pointed at Mr. Falston. His hands began to shake. A quick vision of the smile Mr. Falston wore at the verdict hearing flashed in Trevon's mind. The police siren grew louder.

"Put the gun away," Mr. Falston pleaded. "Just calm down, okay?"

"I came here for a reason!" Trevon took a deep breath.

"Please . . . Don't shoot me!" Mr. Falston threw up his hands then rushed Trevon. Trevon stood his ground. No *justice* . . . no peace. He closed his eyes, pulling back hard on the trigger. Not once, but twice.

Three and a half months later, Trevon found himself back inside the courtroom. Behind him in the packed limited seats sat two women who were his solid source to continue living. Angie and his mother sat in silence as the judge read the verdict.

"Trevon Harrison," Judge Holmes said as he removed his glasses. "It pains me that you felt justice could be carried out by your hands. This system was built to be fair. If your actions were allowed to go unpunished . . . this country would be in utter chaos."

Trevon held his head down, punishing himself by straining his wrist against the handcuffs. Focusing on the pain was better than facing the reality.

When the judge saw that his words were not reaching Trevon, he cleared his throat and asked, "Is there anything you'd like to say before you are sentenced."

The female bailiff helped Trevon to his feet. He glared briefly at the judge with contempt. Silence. When he turned to face his mother and Angie, he did so with his head held up high. He was unable to wipe the tears off his face.

In the third row, Angie and his mother stood. "I—I'm sorry, Momma." He sniffed. "But I can't

have . . . no peace knowing that . . . man . . . what he did to Angie . . . I know Angie told the truth. We both know it."

The bailiff felt pity for Trevon and wiped the falling tears from her eyes. Glancing around the courtroom, she saw a few others reaching up to dry their eyes.

"You said enough, son," his mother said as Angie leaned on her shoulder, sobbing.

"I love you, Momma. You too, lil sis. And remember my promise."

At that moment, Angie broke from her mother's embrace and made a beeline toward Trevon shouting, "DON'T TAKE MY BROTHER AWAY FROM MEEE!"

The understanding bailiff allowed Angie to crush her brother in her arms. The judge grumbled, "I demand order in this court!" The bailiff ignored the judge and motioned Trevon's mother to come and help calm Angie down.

Once order was restored, the judge moved on with the sentencing. "In this judgment, the defendant, Trevon Harrison, having pled guilty to first degree murder, the court orders that he be imprisoned in the Florida Department of Corrections for—"

"Nooooo!" Angie screamed. "That man raped me!

Why won't y'all believe meee!"

"ORDER IN THIS COURT!" Judge Holmes roared and rose to his feet.

Trevon managed to rise to his feet. He did so on his own.

"Bailiff!" Judge Holmes pointed at Angie. "Remove her from my courtroom!"

"I believe you, lil sis!" Trevon shouted. "Always did—and always will!"

Before the day was over, Trevon was sentenced. He begged his family to leave, knowing the system was unfair and would come down hard on him. Trevon kept his head up as Judge Holmes sentenced him to twenty-one years with the possibility of parole.

CHAPTER ONE
August 26, 2011
Friday 10:23 a.m. - Miami, Florida

Thirty-three-year-old Trevon Harrison sat in the back of the non-air conditioned cab. Even with the windows down, it felt like 1,000 degrees and did little to stop the sweat beading up on his baldhead. An irritating drop of sweat and cheap deodorant trickled down his armpit. Even in his discomfort he had a reason to be happy. "We almost dere," the Haitian cab driver said with a hand-rolled cigarette between his cracked lips. "'Nother hot day, huh?"

Trevon nodded. If there was one virtue Trevon had, it was patience.

"Hey!" The cab driver peered at Trevon in the rearview mirror. "Didn't I pick you up—few days ago? Yeah. Took you to the dog track for job," he said.

"A job I didn't get." Trevon leaned up a bit to see the cab driver's ID tag. Through the scratched plexiglass, he saw the cab driver's name. Manuel.

"Why not? What is hard to do dere?"

Trevon shrugged his massive shoulders. "Don't know. Once they heard 'I'm fresh out of prison' I was shown the door."

"Life no fair sometimes," Manuel said, snuffing the cigarette in the ashtray.

"That it ain't," Trevon replied, looking out the window.You look for new job again?"

"Yeah. This will be my sixth interview since I've been out."

"How long you do?"

Trevon glanced down at his hands. "Fifteen years.

Just got out nine days ago."

"You wise to look for job. These streets—" Manuel gestured. "Not the same no more. Young kids wild. Gangs, drugs, nothin' fair no more."

"I feel you on that."

"What type of job you look for?"

"Any job that will keep me gainfully employed. I'll shovel cow shit to avoid going back to prison."

"You on parole?" "Yeah."

"I wish you luck with your effort today. If it not turn out good—" Manuel slid a slot open on the plexiglass and handed Trevon a business card. "I might can get you down at station washing cabs. I put in a good word for you. You seem like nice guy."

"Thanks." Trevon slid the card in his pocket. "Oh, my name is Trevon Harrison."

"Nice to meet ya." Manuel slowed the cab then switched lanes to pass a delivery van.

Trevon's sweat was a mixture of nervousness and anxiety. Adding the relentless Miami heat to the pressure of trying to find a job was slowly taking a toll on Trevon. He was trying hard to do right. Each time he was turned down for a job, it only pushed him to try harder. Angie and his mother were still up in North Carolina, so his support system in Miami was not in his corner. Trevon had left the streets at a young age when he needed support the most. Today, he was a grown man. Most important to him, he was a free grown man. His reason to be happy.

"Ah, here we are my friend," Manuel said, slowing the cab in front of a glass front modern building on Biscayne Boulevard. "Timing good?"

"Perfect," Trevon said then stepped out of the cab.

He reached in his pocket for cab fare.

Leaning across the seat, Manuel shook his head, smiling. "This one on me. Keep your money."

Trevon thanked Manuel then waved at him as he drove off. Trevon stood on the sidewalk as people walked by him. It took only a few seconds to see that he was the only one without a cell phone. Looking up, he had to shield his eyes from the sun. Seven pencil straight palm trees stood in front of the building Trevon was about to enter. Turning around, he waited for an opening in the crowd, then moved closer to the glass mirrored door. He paused a moment to study his reflection. His clothes were casual. Black dress shoes, black cotton pants, and a crisp, white, button-down shirt. His prison built muscular frame was hard to hide. Straightening the collar, he inhaled the sea-scented air, then pulled his pants up an inch. *Please, let me get this job*, he thought.

Reaching the doors, he paused to look at the chrome plated nameplate. Amatory Erotic Films.

Stepping inside the air-conditioned building, he walked up to the security desk. Two stocky white men, both armed, eyed him like a suspect. The smaller of the two guards greeted Trevon with a stern, unsmiling approach.

"Welcome to Amatory Erotic Films. How may I help you?"

"I um, have an eleven o'clock interview with Ms. Babin," Trevon said.

The second guard checked the computer after Trevon told them his name.

"Trevon Harrison, I see it," the second guard replied.

Trevon was asked to show his ID. Once it was fully scrutinized, it was given back along with a visitor's pass that was clipped to his shirt.

"Just head for the elevator and push the button for the third floor, Mr. Harrison." The short guard pointed to the left.

Trevon nodded, then made his way across the soft black carpeted floor. There was no indication that connected the office to an adult film company.

After pressing the button for the elevator, he took a moment to gather his thoughts. *A porn star!* he thought. Under no circumstances was he going back to hustling. Trevon reflected briefly on his past as the elevator began to move. When he gave up his freedom back in '96, he had a side hustle of selling weed and slanging a few small pieces of crack. All done for the strength of his family. His street-earned money placed food on the table and kept the water and power on when his mother was facing hard times making ends meet. Looking at his feet, he hoped he could meet the standards if the chance was given to do a new type of slanging—dick slanging!

The ride up to the third floor was taken alone. When the doors slid open, they revealed a new setting. Everything was white and chrome. Taking a step out, he froze. To his left was a receptionist desk. Behind it sat a cute, young looking black female.

"Welcome to Amatory Erotic Films, Mr. Harrison," the receptionist said with a toothy smile. "Someone will be with you momentarily. You can have a seat to your right." She nodded.

Trevon headed for the cozy waiting lounge. A white horseshoe-shaped leather sofa was the centerpiece. At both ends of the sofa were a few hard core adult magazines on the end tables. The 52-inch flat screen plasma TV was flushed into the wall, currently showing the news. Trevon sat down as the receptionist went back to work. His expectations had not been met. He had assumed the building would be filled with half-naked women prancing around and doing all types of freaky shit. Trevon had come across Amatory Erotic Films by reading an ad in an adult magazine that someone had snuck inside the prison. He only had two years left on his bid when he saw the ad. The fact that Amatory was based in Miami, Florida and not in California had drawn his attention. He leaned over to pick up a magazine when a soft voice called him by his full name. Her accent was definitely Hispanic.

"Trevon Harrison," the woman rolled the letter 'r' as she pronounced his name.

Trevon stood, staring with his mouth agape. The woman was stunningly beautiful. Never during his fifteen-year bid did he think he would be in the presence of a woman of her caliber. He dropped the magazine back on the table as the woman paused to talk to an older female in a cream pantsuit that had gotten off the elevator with her. He cleared his throat as she neared him. Raven black, lustrous curls tumbled past her olive-toned bare shoulders. The clingy colored camisole exposed the cleavage of her succulent breasts with its plunging neckline. Her denim jeans were tight against her juicy appealing thighs, ass and hips. Even in her platform wedge-heeled shoes, she still had to look up to meet his eyes with his 6'4" stance.

"Hi," she said, extending her jeweled wrist and manicured hand. "I'm Jurnee Cruz, Janelle Babin's personal assistant." She shook his large hand, eyeing him openly. She blushed at the size of his arms. They were swollen! His size reminded her of her ex-boyfriend who was a linebacker in the NFL.

Trevon fought hard to keep his eyes from falling into her sea of cleavage. Her top did nothing to hide the size and roundness of her breasts. She had worn the too small camisole without a bra to see how he would react.

"Let's head up to my office," she said, releasing his hand. "Are you nervous?"

"A little bit," he replied, being honest.

They walked beside each other toward the elevator. "That's to be expected," she said, looking at the size of his arms again. "We'll go up to my office and wait until Ms. Babin is ready to see you."

Trevon nodded.

Reaching the elevator, they waited for two black men in business suits to exit. They both greeted Jurnee with a curt nod.

"Up we go," she said, cheerfully ushering Trevon into the elevator. Neither said a word on the short ride up to the sixth floor. When the doors slid open, she stepped out first. Trevon followed and easily allowed his eyes to fall on her round plump ass.

"Care for anything to drink or eat?" she asked over her shoulder.

"I'm good," he said, following her down the hall.

Walking past an office, a skinny white dude stuck his head out and asked Jurnee if she would reply to his e-mail.

"I'll get to it later," she said without looking back or stopping. Nearing the end of the hallway, she stopped at the second to last door on the left. Trevon stood aside as she unlocked the door. Stepping inside, he felt a bit awkward being alone with her once she closed the door. Her office was roomy, with cool warm hues of green painted walls, modern-styled furniture, plush carpet and pictures and awards displayed in a built in wall case. In all four corners sat large tropical potted plants. The huge picture window behind her desk was covered with drapes. He sat down on the green leather bonded couch as she slid behind her desk and into the soft-looking chair.

"So," Jurnee asked, leaning back. "How has your morning been thus far?" She wanted him to be relaxed before meeting the boss.

"Okay," Trevon replied, keeping his eyes on her exotic-looking face. "Just hoping I'll get a chance to um—"

"Have sex with beautiful women on film and get paid for it?" Jurnee stated bluntly.

"Since you put it like that, yeah." Trevon broke into a sheepish grin.

"No need to beat around the bush with me." Jurnee adjusted the camisole over her breasts. "You don't look like you're thirty-three, but I guess the myth is true about prison keeping you looking young."

He shrugged. "It's true in my case, but it ain't true for everyone."

"I'll agree," she said. "But to be honest, I had my doubts about you because of your age."

"Why?"

"Well, in this business, looks are a major asset to success. I'm aware that sex will sell in just about any form. Different people have their lust or fetish for which type of sex they wish to view. I know some men that will only buy hard core DVDs with women featured at two-hundred pounds or better. Women of all shapes and colors can get by. But with men, it can be very selective.

Also, in most films that we produce, the male is the supporting actor. Males are our biggest consumers, so it's only right that we cater to them."

"How do you know so much about porn?" he asked. Jurnee smiled, crossing her shapely legs behind the desk. "I take it that you weren't allowed adult magazines inside prison?"

"I had my fair share. Actually, I had one that had a promo ad for Amatory in it."

She casually brushed a strand of hair out of her face, then reached down to open a drawer on the desk. "My porn name was Honey Drop. And I'm heartbroken that you never heard about me," she teased.

Trevon leaned up to pick up the magazine. Settling back in the couch, his eyes widened. The cover featured Jurnee wearing nothing but a pair of black platform heels and a black leather choker. She was looking back over her shoulder with a finger stuck promiscuously in her mouth. Her naked ass glimmered with oil, looking good enough to eat.

"Y-you-you used to do porn?" he stuttered.

Jurnee nodded up and down. "For nine years." She stood up. "Read the article. I have to use the restroom right quick."

He watched her leave then quickly moved his attention on the magazine. Turning to page twenty-seven, he read up on Jurnee, aka Honey Drop, and what she had accomplished in her nine years of porn. A big surprising fact came when he read that she was forty-one years old. His attention was yanked from the written article after he viewed several hard core pictures from her films. Two small pictures had her with two men. She took one doggy style while filling her mouth with the second. His dick got hard as he viewed each picture of her getting fucked in a number of positions. Adjusting his throbbing erection, he then closed the magazine to calm himself. He had not been with a woman in fifteen years! Trevon was single at the time of his sentencing, so there was no female waiting for him with legs wide open when he was released from prison. He was leaning back with his eyes closed when Jurnee returned.

"Was it that boring?" she asked, easing back behind her desk.

"No." He sat up.

"I was just thinking about something."

"I bet you were." She noticed the magazine on his lap. No doubt, hiding his erection that she was hoping to see. So far his outer appearance had gotten him through the door. Her concern was if Trevon had the *tools* to be a male adult actor. What good was a handsome face and a pussy moistening body with a little dick? Unemployed when it came to Amatory's standards. Jurnee held this thought process in the office as well as in her personal life.

"Why did you show me this?" he asked after she sat down.

"Reason one, I have no shame of my past. Porn to me is liberating. I enjoy having sex, and with me, I'm able to do it without my emotions playing a big part. Reason two, of course, the money and fame was good, but I didn't let them control me."

"So what do you do now?"

"You forgot already." She laughed. "I'm Ms. Babin's assistant—remember?"

"Oh, yeah." He looked down at the magazine and held it up. "So you're really done with porn?"

"One hundred percent, if you're asking if I get in front of the camera."

"How does your man feel about you being a former adult film actress?"

Jurnee laughed, she knew this question was coming. "I didn't mention anything about being in a relationship in that interview you just read, and as the saying goes . . ." She held up her left hand showing no ring. "I've had my share of relationships. I prefer being single."

"Do you have any regrets about doing porn?"

"Nope," she said, glancing at her watch. "I'll share this with you. Many men have high hopes of being a porn star. It's not an easy job. If you think it's all about getting your dick hard and ramming it in and out of a willing female, then you'll be in for a big surprise. You'll have to act. You'll have to sell yourself to the camera. Think you can stop in mid-stroke of the director's cue? Think you'll be able to get hard in a room with ten or more faces focused on you? I'm not trying to discourage you. I'm just telling you the true facts of this business."

"I guess I have much to learn."

"Just be willing to learn and listen and you'll go far in this business. You can trust me on that." Jurnee winked.

"Okay, since you know everything that goes on in this business, what can you tell me to keep in my mind as a golden rule?"

"A golden rule you ask?" She thought for a minute. "One that you hold the closest."

"This is all assuming you'll be signed to Amatory, right?"

"Call it positive thinking," he said, grinning. "Well." She smiled. "If you're signed, I'll tell you

my golden rule. But right now, I need to get you up to see the boss lady."

"What do I call her? Janelle or Ms. Babin?"

"Ms. Babin. And with her, it would be a good idea too."

"Can I keep this?" He stood up with the magazine. "Sure." Jurnee winked as he tucked it under his arm. "You can leave that here and come back and get it after your interview, okay?"

Walking down the hall toward the elevator, he enjoyed the backshot. Her ass was soft looking, making him want to squeeze it. The temptation was strong, but Trevon was able to beat it. Reaching the elevator, she boldly reached up to fix his collar. He had no choice but to gaze at her breasts. She showed no protest as he looked.

"There." She smiled. "Perfect."

"Thanks," he muttered, wishing he could spend more time with her.

"Okay. This is where we part. When you get up to Janelle's floor, just step over to the receptionist desk and she'll take care of you. And be yourself, okay?"

"I will," he said as the elevator doors parted.

She took a step back and waved playfully as the doors slid shut. Pulling out her Smartphone, she made a quick call to the receptionist on Janelle's floor.

"Ruby. Hi, this is Jurnee. If you see Kandi up there tell her to come to my office. It's urgent."

Karma 3:
Beast of Burden

Tash Hawthorne

This is a work of fiction. Names, characters, places, and incidents either are the product of the author's imagination or are used fictitiously, and any resemblance to actual persons, living or dead, business establishments, events, or locales are entirely coincidental.

Wahida Clark Presents Publishing
60 Evergreen Place
Suite 904A
East Orange, New Jersey 07018
1(866)-910-6920
www.wclarkpublishing.com

Copyright 2018 © by Tash Hawthorne

All rights reserved. This book, or parts thereof, may not be reproduced in any form without permission.

Library of Congress Cataloging-In-Publication Data:
Tash Hawthorne
Karma 3: Beast of Burden
ISBN 13-digit 978-1-9477322-6-1 (paper)
ISBN 13-digit 978-1-9477322-8-5 (ebook)

Library of Congress Catalog Number 2018906370
1. Urban, Contemporary, Women, African-American, Cuban-American – Fiction

Cover design and layout by Nuance Art, LLC
Book design by NuanceArt@aCreativeNuance.com
Edited by Linda Wilson
Proofreader Rosalind Hamilton

Printed in USA

Prologue

A "News at Noon" logo zooms across the screen with the ABC7 logo, current time and date set in the bottom right corner.

"We're going to shift gears now," an Asian-American news anchor says. "Former Newark police officer Money Parks was released from prison Monday after serving fifteen years for the attempted murder of his infant son."

The news camera cuts to video footage of Money walking away from his former domicile and toward a waiting car.

"I'm eager to get reacquainted with my family and reconnect severed relationships . . . apologize for what I've put them through," the former officer said through his lawyer. "Start my life over with God being first and the center of everything I do."

The news camera cuts back to the Asian-American anchor.

"In 2008, a day after the child turned one-year-old, Parks shot his infant son in the back while he was sleeping. Parks pleaded volitional insanity, a defense of irresistible impulse, which asserts that the defendant, although able to distinguish right from wrong at the time of the act, suffers from a mental illness or defect that makes him or her incapable of controlling his or her actions. His lawyer said he has since been treated for his mental illness, gone through counselling, and taught Bible study. The shooting marked the start of a cascade of troubles for Parks, who was promptly suspended from his job as a decorated Newark police officer. He lost custody of his daughter from a previous relationship, his mother died five years after his conviction, and he was accused of assaulting a guard with a deadly weapon upon learning the news of his mother's death. The mother of the baby whom Parks shot, Olympic gold medallist, Karma Alonso-Walker could not be reached for comment."

An aged hand places a bottle of alcohol to its lips. The 46-inch television screen fades to black. A pair of brown eyes peer into the oversized black monitor. A chestnut brown reflection stares back. A white bottle of pills jiggles in another aged hand. Nostrils flare. Swollen fingers ball into fists.

Chapter 1

Karma heard the panic in her son's voice as he bellowed, "Mom!"

"Mekhi, what's the matter?" Karma asked. "Mom! Papa said he can't breathe!" he uttered.

"What?" Karma struggled to hear her son over the loud music and video game sound effects in the background. "Mekhi! Turn the TV down!" She slid to the edge of her seat.

"He can't breathe! He's sweating and, and—"

"Call nine-one-one, Mekhi! I'll be right there!" she assured him, rising from her chair. Karma slammed the phone down, snatched her coat and purse off the coat rack, and ran out of the office.

"*Tio!*" she shouted, running through the dining hall toward the kitchen. "*Tio!*"

Miguel looked up from the prep station and stopped dicing an onion. He immediately noticed the alarm in his niece's voice. He retrieved a cloth from the pocket of his apron and cleaned his hands with it while meeting Karma at the service station.

"*Que pasa?*" he asked.

"Mekhi called. Something's wrong with my father," she informed him, zipping up her coat. "Okay. Go, go," he insisted.

"*Le llamaré!*" she yelled over her shoulder as she raced out the door of her restaurant.

* * * * *

Lorenzo lay crumpled on the floor in the fetal position when she entered the house. She'd expected to see paramedics and Mekhi, but neither was in attendance. In that moment, Karma realized Mekhi hadn't called them at all. Her father's head was resting in a pool of vomit, his body seizing, and creating a steady knocking sound against the wooden floor beneath him. The sight before her stopped her breath momentarily. It was the second time she'd found one of her parents in a horrific state on the floor.

Not again, she thought. *No . . . no.* Karma snapped out of her entranced state and ran over to her father. "Mekhi?" she yelled. "Mekhi?" *Where is Mekhi?* Karma threw herself onto her knees, snatched her wool scarf from around her neck, and placed it under his head.

"Daddy? Daddy!" she screamed. "Please. Please, don't do this to me!" Karma frantically reached into her pea coat pocket and retrieved her cell phone. She dialled 911.

"Nine-one-one, what's your emergency?" a woman with a husky voice breathed through the line.

"I need an ambulance to come to 598 Elmwynd Drive in Orange, New Jersey. My father's having a seizure," Karma responded hysterically, as she wiped the sweat off her father's face.

"Where is your father located, ma'am?" she asked calmly.

"He's on the floor in the living room. I'm with him," Karma replied, holding his face in her hands.

"How long has he been seizing?" the operator implied. "I-I-I don't know. My son called me while I was at work.

I-I just got here a couple of minutes ago." *Mekhi.* Karma's wild, honey-brown eyes scoured the room for her son. *Where is he?*

"Okay, ma'am. If he is not already on his side, carefully roll him onto—" she began.

"He's already on his side!" Karma stressed.

"Okay, good. Are his eyes rolled back into his head?"

Karma zoomed in on the windows to the soul of the man whom she loved and hated, feared and fought. His lids fluttered. The whites of his eyes were visible,; nothing more, nothing less.

"Yes!" Karma bellowed.

Suddenly, the rocking stopped. The room became silent. Lorenzo was still. Karma's untamed eyes widened, and she immediately searched her father's face for life. His eyes were still lost and his mouth--——-agape.

"Daddy? Daddy?" Karma cried. Tears flooded her eyes as the vision of her brutally beaten mother came into view, clouding the image of her father before her.

"Ma'am . . . Ma'am," the operator called.

"Daddy? Daddy?" She rolled him over onto his back. "He's not breathing! Daddy?"

"He's stopped breathing?" the woman asked, innocently.

"He's not breathing!" Karma replied, hysterically .

THIRSTY

A novel by

MIKE SANDERS

This is a work of fiction. Names, characters, places, and incidents either are the product of the author's imagination or are used fictitiously, and any resemblance to actual persons, living or dead, business establishments, events, or locales is entirely coincidental.

Wahida Clark Presents Publishing, LLC
60 Evergreen Place
Suite 904
East Orange, New Jersey 07018
1(866)910-6920
www.WClarkPublishing.com

Copyright 2008 © by Mike Sanders.

All rights reserved. This book, or parts thereof, may not be reproduced in any form without permission.

Thirsty
ISBN 13-digit 978-0-9818545-4-0 (Paperback)
ISBN 10-digit 0-9818545-4-0
ISBN 13-digit 978-1-944992-35-4 (Hardback)
ISBN 10-digit 1-9449923-5-9
ISBN 13-digit 978-1-936649-83-9 (Ebook)
Library of Congress Catalog Number 2009921479

1. Urban, Charlotte, North Carolina, Hip-Hop, Women, African American, – Fiction
Cover design and layout by Baja Wakiri Ukweli
Book design by Jonathan Gullery
Edits and layout by Nuance Art.*.
www.DesignsByNuance.com
order@acreativenuance.com

Printed in United States

PROLOGUE
JUSTICE

As I nervously climbed those winding stairs with my baby .380 clutched tightly in my sweaty palms, I could feel beads of sweat trickling

down between my breasts. With each step I climbed, my heart beat like jungle drums and felt as if it would leap from my chest at any given moment. Regardless, I knew I had to still my nerves, but I also knew there was no turning back! I'd decided that *today* would be the day I'd make this nigga pay for all of the pain and anguish he'd put me through.

As I neared the door to his home office I could hear the familiar melodious sound of his money counting machine as it rhythmically spit out bill after bill. I was hoping that I'd rocked him to sleep during our time together so he'd be totally oblivious to what I was about to do. I was also hoping that he'd gotten so comfortable as to have left the door unlocked. He knew I had never disturbed him while he was in this room handling his business because I knew a man needed his space from time to time. But today, *his* space was about to become *mine* as well.

When I was directly in front of the large, oak door I stood there and silently prayed my nerves would allow me to carry out my task. Hell, it's not everyday a sistahh's about to catch a damn *body*!

A million and one emotions began to well up in me all at once. So suddenly, that it felt as if they were colliding and toppling over one another. I tried with all the restraint I could muster up to hold back the tears, which were fighting to be released, but it was to no avail. My eyes lost the battle and the water sprang free. Mascara streaked down my chiseled cheekbones as the tears flowed freely.

Just the thought of how easily the man beyond this door had come into my life and turned it upside down, made me really grasp the concept of what could happen when a man catches you at a vulner- able stage. I witnessed first hand how a woman's mind can really get twisted.

After taking a deep, nervous breath I reached for the cold knob and was thoroughly surprised to find it *unlocked*. I paused for a moment to muster up the courage I needed. With a trembling hand, I twisted the brass knob and hurriedly pushed the heavy door open just in time witness this nigga's eyes almost pop out of their sockets as he looked up from his desk where he sat.

"Justice," he called out my name while staring in astonishment as I stood there in his doorway brandishing a pistol, looking like a crazed woman.

CHAPTER ONE

How It All Began…

Located downtown on South Summit Avenue was club Nine Three Five, and everybody who was somebody was up in the house tonight.

Charlotte's hottest nightclub was off the hook for its first annual "Grown & Sexy White Party." All patrons were dressed immaculately from head to toe in all white. From a distance it looked angelic. It was showtime for real. Dope boys competing with the celebrities and the girls competing with each other.

DJ Incognito was pumping the latest Mary J. Blige hit. The sound of the bass invaded my soul as I sat slightly swaying my hips on the barstool and observing the packed mirrored dance floor. The whole while I was keeping a close eye on the VIP.

Carolina Panthers' Julius Peppers held down the VIP section with several of his teammates along with a few members of the Charlotte Bobcats basketball team. Panthers' star wide receiver Steve Smith was celebrating his birthday and champagne was flowing like it was mere tap water. Security was thick like Obama himself was trying to get a drink. But that didn't stop the hundreds of groupies from begging for VIP wristbands and trying to get in. Charlotte's most elite nightclub was packed to capacity and it was a wonder that the fire marshals hadn't yet come and tried to shut things down.

It is a known fact that whenever the ballers came out to party, so does the "baller chasers." Needless to say, every chick who thought they had what it took to snag one of those niggas was hovering around the club in the skimpiest outfit they could squeeze into, lurking like vultures waiting for the kill.

Money attracts women, so for every one male there were at least three women and the men were taking complete advantage of the three to one ratio. Most of the men were well groomed and looked as if they had just stepped out of the barber's chair. But there were a few who looked like they had just finished going ten rounds with Mike Tyson. Most of these niggas were hustlers whose chips were not stacked as high as the ball players, yet and still, together they flossed enough ice to build a three-family igloo.

My girl Sapphire and I were seated at one of the two bars on the first level of the club basking in the limelight. We were enjoying our drinks and grooving to the smooth sounds that were pouring from the sound system. I was in my zone and feeling hella good! Guys had been checkin' for us all night, but Sapphire and I were unfazed by all of the attention we had been receiving. One by one, we had been shooting niggas down left and right. But that didn't deter a few who were still relentlessly determined to holla. Evidently, quite a few seem- ingly assumed they had what the next man didn't because even well into the night they were still approaching.

We hadn't been out in quite some time so we were truly letting it all hang out tonight. Being the object of most men's desire was nothing new to us. We were accustomed to stealing away most of the other chicks' spotlights wherever we went. This night was no different.

Sapphire and I were what most people would refer to as *mysteries* because no one really knew a whole lot about us. Men *loved* us because they couldn't have us at the drop of a hat like most other chicks, and women *hated* us because they couldn't figure us out. The hate never really bothered us because we were aware of the fact that it is human nature for us to fear and oftentimes hate what we don't understand. For that reason, our circle always stayed as tight as a nun's pussy. Besides the two of us, we didn't have any female friends because bitches are just *too* jealous.

As I swiveled around on my stool to face the bar I was startled by a presence that had sidled his way between me and Sapphire. Evidently, this nigga had spoken to me while I was checking out the VIP, but I hadn't heard a word he'd said.

"What!? I can't hear you," I shouted over the loud music to, yet, another brother whom had invaded me and my girl's space for what seemed like the umpteenth time since our arrival at the club. This one definitely had no chance whatsoever. His face was decorated with the kind of pimples I hadn't seen since junior high school and his so-called dreads were so matted up they looked like a throw rug. The instant deal breaker was his dental work. He was displaying my ultimate turn-off—platinum teeth! I hate to see metal in a grown man's mouth.

"I said can I buy the beautiful lady a drink?" Dreadlocks repeated himself slightly louder than he'd done the first time.

"No thank you, sweetie. I'm straight," I replied casually, trying not to be rude. I picked up my XO from the bar and took a sip just to make sure he saw that I had a fresh drink and didn't need his assistance. Dreadlocks kept trying to holla but I had already tuned him out after the word "drink" had escaped his lips. I was so not feeling this nigga! I turned my back to him and started talking to Sapphire while he stood there looking angry and dejected.

"Oh, so you gonna just turn ya' back to a nigga while he talkin' to you?" Dreadlocks asked with his burnt lips a little too close to my ear. He was so close I could feel one of his dreads grazing my neck. I could also smell his breath, which reeked of alcohol and cigarettes.

At this point I felt as if Dreadlocks was being a slight bit disrespectful. This caused the tiny steel ball in the center of my tongue to start clacking against the insides of my top front teeth. Clacking my tongue ring was a predisposition that happened anytime I'm angry or annoyed. And it happened every time without fail!

I continued to ignore him until he finally got the message that I wasn't going to give him any rhythm. He sauntered off in search of another potential victim. But not before calling me a "conceited bitch."

"Ooooooh, no-the-hell-he-didn't!" Sapphire commented in disbelief as she watched the guy walk away. "Rude ass nigga. Right up your alley, huh, Justice," she teased with a pearly white smile. Her soft voice was straining to be heard over the roaring music.

"Bitch, pleeze. Smelled like he had a lil' man wit' shitty boots on walking around in the back of his throat. I almost passed-the-fuck- out!" I had my nose turned up as if I could still smell the guy's breath. Sapphire and I always got a kick out of teasing one another. We were the *shit* and we knew it. It had once been stated that, "A beautiful woman armed with a load of confidence is considered to be a dangerous woman!" Me and my girl definitely oozed with exuberant confidence.

We were two bitches with class, sass, *and* ass! A helluva combination.

I sat my drink down and glanced over at the mirror behind the bar where the liquor was stacked and caught a glimpse of my reflection. I was dressed in a pair of leather Dolce & Gabbana white shorts that accented my well toned butter scotch thighs and a silk blouse that was unbuttoned down to the crease of my breasts. I wasn't wearing a bra, so I knew men would be drooling over my perky breasts every time the silk shirt grazed my nipples.

With one fluid motion I uncrossed, then crossed my legs again, placing the opposite leg atop the other so all of the lustful-eyed niggas could get a quick flash of thick thighs. I also did it so all of the jealous chicks that I knew were watching could get a good look at my expensive Guiseppe stiletto thong boots.

I looked over at Sapphire and saw her give me one of those, "Gurl, you a damn trip" looks as she twisted her lips into a half-smile because she knew exactly what I was doing. Not wanting to be outdone, Sapphire flipped her jet-black shoulder length tresses backwards over her shoulder so the platinum diamond earrings she was wearing could sparkle for everyone to see. She glanced down at her cleavage and discreetly adjusted her ample ebony D-cups so that they looked as if they were about to pop out of the top of the white Prada dress with spaghetti straps. As I watched my girl vie for attention, for the first time that night I noticed how well the dress she had chosen to wear was clashing perfectly with her chocolate skin.

Although Sapphire is a pound or two slimmer than my voluptuous frame she is still a far cry from being petite. Nor does she have my slanted eyes, but she is still as fine as wine in her own right. On a daily basis I continuously get compared to that Kimora Lee chick because of my "Asian-like" eyes and the uncanny resemblance we bare. Sapphire on the other hand had been told a time or two that she could pass for a thicker version of Gabrielle Union—all the way down to the dimples. While grooving on my stool to Anthony Hamilton's latest joint, I unconsciously thought about how much my girl Sapphire has meant to me for years. I conceded that she was truly the sister I never had. Although I loved my friend to death, there were times when she could be a tad bit nerve wracking with her naïveté. At this time, I was twenty- two, only nineteen months older than Sapphire. However, that age gap seemed so much broader because I'd been exposed to so much more shit.

I had never really lived what one would call a sheltered life and I've always had street smarts. There's absolutely nothing slow about me but the way I walk. Therefore, sometimes it took a true vet such as myself to school Sapphire on certain aspects of life, especially when it came to trifling ass men. Nevertheless, no matter how many times I would try to tell her about those dogs, she would fail to take heed; leading her to a broken heart every other week.

For example, a few weeks ago Sapphire had caught her so-called boyfriend Travis getting his tiny ass dick sucked by her cousin. Her trifling ass first cousin Joy had been on her knees giving him dome in his living room while he sat there on the sofa with his pants around his ankles. He hadn't even had the common sense to take the liberty of locking the damn door when he knew Sapphire could pop up at any given moment. I would have kicked both their asses. She just calmly walked back down the steps to the parking lot and keyed his Benz.

I had even tried to warn Sapphire that Travis's dog ass was no damn good and how he had even had the audacity to try me when she was not around. However, Sapphire wouldn't listen and had to find out the hard way.

Nevertheless, I have always felt compassion for my girl. The two of us had been as thick as thieves for years.

We had met years earlier when my mother had moved me and my younger brother Monk to Charlotte, North Carolina, from Chicago in search of a "better life," so she had said.

When our family had first arrived in Charlotte we ended up living next door to Sapphire and her mother in Piedmont Courts housing projects (one of the worst projects in the city at that time). Sapphire's mother and my mother became friends, so naturally, Sapphire and I spent a lot of time together. Back then Sapphire's mother had an abusive boyfriend named Ty and I often noticed bruises on Sapphire's arms and legs, which she always claimed to come from falling or bumping into things. School counselors also noticed and questioned her, but she continuously convinced them that nothing was wrong at home.

One night Sapphire's mother and Ty were arguing so loud that it woke me up out of my sleep. Next thing I heard was a gunshot followed by shrill screams. Two minutes later, Sapphire's mother was banging on our door, screaming and crying hysterically. She was yelling that Ty had shot himself. She was trembling so hard that she couldn't have dialed 911 if she had tried. So, my mother called the police for her.

I was sitting up in my bed, listening to my mother try to calm Sapphire's mother down when my bedroom door slowly opened. Sapphire stood there in her bed clothes. Her eyes were lifeless and she looked like she had seen a damn ghost. I got up and pulled her into my room and shut the door.

"What happened?" I asked.

She didn't respond. I think she was in shock.

Sapphire finally climbed into bed with me like she always did when- ever she spent the night. She curled up into a ball and just stared up at the ceiling. My nosey ass wanted to know what had happened to Ty, but Sapphire was not telling. The next morning it was all over the news and all over the neighborhood that Ty had shot himself in the head. It was ruled a suicide. But later that day, after my best friend made me promise to never repeat what she was about to tell me, Sapphire broke down and told me what *really* happened.

Ty had been molesting Sapphire for two years right up under her mother's nose. Sapphire wouldn't tell because he had said he'd kill her and her mother if anyone ever found out, and she believed him. The night he died Sapphire's mother had caught him sneaking out of Sapphire's room and zipping up his pants. An argument ensued and Sapphire's mother asked her what Ty was doing in her room. Sapphire finally told on him. Sapphire's mother must've temporarily lost her mind and went to get Ty's gun from their bedroom drawer. She blew his brains out right before Sapphire's young eyes.

For all these years I've kept my promise to my girl and no one will ever know about that night unless she told them because I intended to take her secret to my grave!

Ever since Sapphire had caught Travis she had been a little down in the dumps. So, I figured a night out at Nine Three Five was just what the doctor ordered to get her mind off of things.

"Look," said Sapphire while nodding toward the dance floor. "Shabba Ranks still tryin' to get at you." She was referring to the guy who had called me a "conceited bitch."

I turned towards the dance floor and spotted Dreadlocks dancing with a heavyset light-skinned chick. He was staring at me with blood-shot eyes. I held his gaze for a second, then sat my drink on the bar and raised my right hand to my lips. I blew a kiss in his direction while displaying my best fake smile.

Sapphire took a sip of her Mimosa and almost chocked when she saw what I'd just done. She choked back a cough and wiped her lips with a napkin.

"Why the hell you do that? You know he gonna come runnin' his lil' happy ass back over here."

"I want him to catch that and kiss my ass wit' it. I got his 'conceited bitch'," I replied while picking my drink back up and resumed to sip and groove.

"O-Kaaay," Sapphire teased as we both laughed and raised our hands high for a high-five, then commenced to slap hands in midair.

I looked around the smoke-filled room and saw several big time hustlers. Some I recognized, others were new faces. They were all sipping champagne and trying to holla at anybody who they thought would fall victim to their prowess. My eyes wandered to one of the many pool tables in a far corner of the room where two fine ass brothers were shooting a game. It was obvious to me that they were not ball players because they just had that "street" appeal that made my spine tingle. The jewels they were draped in were shining so brightly I could see the sparkle of different colored stones even from where I was seated. It's safe to say that they looked very appetizing.

However, I had to check myself because I'd sworn off fucking with hustlers. I absolutely refused to go down that avenue again. I'd had entirely too many close brushes with danger while fucking with those types of men in my past. I must admit though, I definitely enjoyed the benefits I'd reaped from playing my role with them, but the reward was not worth the risk.

Back in the day I had never really understood why most women were always attracted to the niggas who would have rather hugged the streets than hug their woman. That chronicle had always been somewhat a mystery to me until one day I met a street nigga named

Carlos who turned my ass out! Had me running behind him and even searching for his ass in broad daylight with a flashlight. Had a bitch sprung.

I had met Carlos at a nightclub downtown in the Adam's Mark hotel a few years back and it had been on since the day I first laid eyes on him. He was the only man who could handle me and my wild ways. He kept me laced in the latest fashions and I never wanted for anything when I was with him. But I got tired of being so dependent on him and wanted my own shit and he didn't like that. That's when the problems started and we ended up going our separate ways. We stayed cool, but it was never like it was in the beginning of our relationship.

Since dealing with Carlos, I had begun to understand why a woman would act that way over those types of niggas. But for the life of me I still couldn't seem to explain it. Personally, there was just something about a nigga dressed in baggy jeans with a mean swagger and a perma- nent screw faced expression that made my thong sticky upon first sight. And God forbid if the nigga had a baldhead, I'd have to wring my panties out like a wet dish cloth. Like a fool, I thought I could change a hustler. That is, until I began to see a continuous pattern of those men eventually changing *me*. Since I'd reformed from getting seriously involved with street niggas I still couldn't let go of the sex. I absolutely had to have me some of that "thug dick" from time to time.

It's true what they say about thugs. They've got the best dick game! Whoever had coined the phrase "thug love" must have had experienced some of that same "I can't walk straight 'cause dis nigga done fucked me 'til my pussy was raw" type sex that I've endured with a few street niggas, especially with my ex Carlos. Sex between the two of us had always been earth shattering!

Lately I'd been setting my sights higher and I was determined

to make my dollars graduate. For instance, all of those ball playing niggas who were in the club tonight were all fair game. A little challenge has never hurt anyone before. Besides, I have always been thirsty for guap, a thirst that will never be quenched.

I finally looked away from the pool table where the hustlers were and fixed my gaze on the dance floor, then over to the second bar area hoping to spot a potential victim. No one caught my eye. I then gazed toward the area where the VIP was located and saw the familiar faces of several well-known athletes who were surrounded by groupies. While observing these tricks, I sucked my teeth and rolled my eyes at those cheap ass hookers who were fucking the game up for "real" bitches such as myself. I knew half of those heifers would fuck for a mere buck and the other half would do something real strange for a little piece of change. They had no idea how to get real money from those niggas. That thought alone had me seething with anger.

Sapphire must have did a CAT scan on my brain and read my thoughts. "Girl, what you over there thinkin' 'bout?" she asked.

"See that." I pointed towards the VIP area. "It's hoes like that who be in the way and blockin'."

Sapphire turned on her stool in the direction in which I was looking.

She teased, "Don't hate. Participate."

"Chile pleeze. Them hoes can't even smell my panties, let alone fuck wit' my game. I'll run circles around them square ass bitches."

I looked at my girl and realized she didn't have a clue as to how treacherous I was.

I thought, *If you only knew.*

A little while later, the drinks I had consumed throughout the evening had finally begun to catch up with me. I felt my bladder expand a little. Tiny beads of sweat began forming on my forehead indicating that I was a little tipsy. I reached for a napkin on the bar, dabbed my forehead and decided that now was as good a time as any to make that dreaded trip to the ladies' room.

"Watch my drink. Gotta tinkle," I told Sapphire as I grabbed my Chloe handbag from the bar and rose to my feet. As soon as I had stood up I realized I had a better buzz than I'd originally thought. When the lightheadedness finally subsided I headed towards the restroom, which seemed as if it was a mile away. I got stopped by at least six different guys while en route. While fanning my way through the thick clouds of cigarette and cigar smoke I only said "Hi" and kept it moving. It was hard as hell still trying to be cute while I was about to piss on myself.

The bright lights in the bathroom helped me shake a little of my high off. Surprisingly, the bathroom was clean despite so much traffic in and out all night. Even the air didn't smell half bad inside. I guessed all of the trifling chicks had stayed home this night.

After finally relieving my aching bladder I decided to touch up my lip-gloss and reapply my mascara. While in the mirror minding my business I saw two of the groupies come sauntering in. They were the main two I'd seen hanging all over the ball players in VIP. The two girls, one high yellow and the other pecan tan, were visibly twisted.

The skirts they both wore were so short you could see a hint of ass cheeks hanging out. Apparently they had no shame whatsoever because they began bragging candidly about how they were going to meet up with two of the football players at the Embassy Suites hotel after the club. They even mentioned room numbers. I didn't know if the two girls were trying to impress me or if they were just that oblivious to my presence. But I managed to keep my game face on and was filing all of that pertinent info away in my mental rolodex.

The groupies were in the middle of discussing stopping by the Waffle House before joining the players at the room when I'd decided I'd heard enough. I was packing up my things and getting ready to leave the restroom when I saw the high yellow chick pour a line of coke onto a compact mirror and they both shared a hit. Afterwards, they engaged in a passionate uninhibited kiss. Other chicks were coming in and out of the restroom and acted as if the two girls' actions were normal. No one commented, no one stared.

"Dust head, dyke bitches," I muttered under my breath in disgust as I began to make my exit. My mind was doing cartwheels and somer- saults and my mental cash register began *cha-chinging* like crazy. Only if those girls could have read my thoughts at that instance. My devious mind was working full-throttle!

I left the two groupies in the restroom and headed back to my seat at the bar. I almost managed to make it back without too much harass- ment from the hardheads. That shit is so annoying. As soon as I made it back to my seat, I saw Sapphire's trifling ass cousin Joy and one of her girlfriends approaching the bar area near where we were seated. I nudged Sapphire with my elbow and nodded in Joy's direction so that she could take notice. When Sapphire spotted her cousin, I saw fire jump into her eyes. I was halfway hoping she would take out her earrings and slap some Vaseline on her face old school style and beat that hoe down. But for the moment Sapphire managed to maintain her composure.

Joy sashayed her narrow ass over to where we were seated. The baggy pants suit she was wearing seemed to swallow her small frame. The shoes she had on were so ran down it looked as if she had been running track in them. Her micro braids were frizzy as hell and her eyes held that glossy, ex induced look. Just one glance is all it took for me to tell that she was "rollin'." Her big-boned girlfriend was right behind her looking twice as jacked up as Joy was.

Joy looked at me and rolled her eyes with one hand on her skinny ass hips and the other clutching a half-empty Heineken bottle. She turned to Sapphire and before she could fix her mouth to speak, Sapphire spat, "If you ain't comin' to tell a bitch that your triflin' ass got the Ebola virus and finna die within the next twenty-four hours I suggest you not open your mouth! 'Cause I don't feel like hearing *shit* you gotta say! 'Cause I'm about two seconds off your ass! I really feel like gettin' all up in yo' bizness right about now!"

It was obvious that Sapphire was having flashbacks of walking in on Joy sucking Travis's dick. And the more she thought about it the more heated she became.

Joy stood there with a dumbfounded expression glued to her face while Big Boned stood behind her looking like she had something to say. I sat there stunned because I had never seen Sapphire this heated before, but I guess she had good reason to be. The way she was looking all fiery-eyed and screw faced almost led me to believe she was about to invite Joy out to the parking lot. She knew I had my "baby .380" in the car, and judging from the size of this chick Joy had with her, we would have definitely needed it for her swole ass. Besides, I was just *too* cute that night to be taking an ass whippin'.

Joy looked at Sapphire with a scowl and turned to walk away.

Before she walked off she stated a defiant "Fuck you!"

Hearing this, Sapphire rolled her neck ghetto-style and returned, "Nah, fuck *you!* You bum bitch!" Sapphire put her drink down and started to rise up off her stool. I grabbed her arm and stopped her. I looked around and saw that we were getting a few unwanted, inquisitive stares from individuals who had evidently heard the berating between the two cousins and were undoubtedly expecting a catfight.

After Joy and her friend had left I tried to calm Sapphire down. I patted her thigh and said, "Girl, fuck Joy. She can't help it that she's a nympho. All that bitch think about is dick. Dick, dick, dick. If it ain't on her mind, it's in her mouth."

Sapphire looked at me sideways.

"Okay, bad choice of words. But you know what I mean. Let that bitch have sloppy seconds. You know she wasn't doin' nothing but tastin' you when she was suckin' Travis's dick."

I watched Joy as she snaked her way through the crowd.

"Up in here lookin' a hot ass mess," I added as I saw Sapphire trying to surpress a smile. I could tell she was lightening up a little.

"I know right? Did you see the shoes that hoe had on?" Sapphire added as we shared a small laugh.

A few minutes later, the atmosphere had calmed down a little. I looked over at Sapphire and tried to figure out where that sudden violent streak had emerged. Ever since I'd known Sapphire she had always been the cool, peaceful type. Only this night I saw something in her that made me look at her in a totally different light. I thought for a moment that maybe my girl was finally ready to get down with my hustle and roll with a bitch. Then on second thought, I rational- ized that she was not yet ready to jump out there with an ocean full of sharks. For the simple fact that some of the shit I was into was so devious and conniving that it had my own conscience fucked up at times. I concluded that she was definitely not ready.

While I was in deep thought I happened to see the same two groupies from the restroom saying their goodbyes to the players. I couldn't quite figure out which two of the players they had planned their rendezvous with but then again, it really didn't matter because they all had dough, and I definitely wanted some of it.

"Gotta go do somethin' right quick. Be right back," I told Sapphire as I fished my phone out of my purse and quickly headed toward the club's exit.

Once outside, I stood a few feet away from the exit door and punched in digits on my cell. I was trying my best to ignore the "Yo, ma" and "What up, shorty" from the niggas who were milling around and loitering. They truly acted as if they had a lack of anything better to do.

I stood on the curb with my phone glued to my ear and my eyes were trained on the club's exit waiting for the two groupies to emerge. I was hoping they'd come right out behind me so I wouldn't have to be outside too long. Although it was still summer, the night air was chilly and my arms were starting to form chill bumps.

I listened as the line rang three times before it was eventually answered. Coincidentally, as soon as the line was answered I spotted the two chicks coming out of the club giggling and staggering slightly. As I watched them stroll through the parking lot, I spoke into my phone. I kept my eyes on them until they reached their car, a late model Honda Accord. That was all I needed to see. I then turned my attention away from them and resumed my conversation.

After a few minutes of idle chatter I finally ended the call with my younger brother Monk and attempted to re-enter the club. Just before I reached the entrance I felt a hand on my arm. The vulgar comments and crazy ass looks from niggas I could deal with, but putting your hands on me without my permission is a straight-up violation!

Instinctively, I spun around with all intentions of checkin' whoever this nigga was that had the audacity to put his hands on me. I turned on my heels with my mouth open, ready to go off. However, I was repressed when I came face to face with one of the finest pieces of masculinity I'd ever seen! My demeanor immediately softened as I blinked twice in succession to make sure my eyes weren't playing tricks on me and to make sure the liquor didn't have a sistah hallucinating.

The first thing I noticed was his complexion. His skin looked as if someone had dipped him into a bowl of creamy chocolate, then sat his ass out in the sun to dry. I was loving that! Purely out of habit, starting with his shoes I gave his attire a quick once-over as my eyes scanned his body like a bar code. He had on spotless white on white Prada sneakers and Mek jeans. He also had on a button-down shirt that was unbut- toned, revealing a broad chest covered by a white tee. I couldn't even front, I was feeling his appearance. I realized that he must not been inside the club because he wasn't wearing what the dress code had required. I wouldn't have been able to miss all of *that* up in there anyway.

He looked to be at least six-three because I stand at five-seven without heels and this night my heels had four inches on them. Even with the heels on he was still towering over me by at least three inches. And, oh-my-God, his head was as smooth as a baby's naked ass! "Excuse me, can I have a minute?" His voice boomed with so much

baritone-like bass that it made my nipples tighten up!

I wanted to say "A minute? Hell, for you I got a whole lifetime." However, I folded my arms across my suddenly erect nipples and responded, "Maybe. Depends."

I was demurely biting my bottom lip, trying my damnest to look sexy while continuing to hold his gaze.

He flashed a Taye Diggs-like smile displaying even, pearly whites, then he casually stroked his well-trimmed goatee before extending his hand to me

"I'm J.T."

"Justice," I blurted out. Then I flinched at the realization that I'd just given him my real name. That was something I very rarely did upon first introduction.

Damn I'm slippin', I thought as I allowed him to take my hand. He raised it to his luscious lips and blessed it with the most seductive kiss I'd ever felt. I had to shake my head in an attempt to snap out of the spell this nigga had put me under.

This nigga got a bitch straight trippin'.

I took back possession of my hand while further observing this Adonis in human form standing before me. Because of his height I concluded that he was probably a "hoop nigga." Then on second guess, the edginess he was exuding screamed "street nigga." I had really been trying to leave those types of niggas alone, but J.T. had my ass ready to backslide!

While we were having our moment, a jet-black Hummer with a set of big ass chrome rims pulled alongside us and stopped. The windows were so heavily tinted the only thing I could see was quick flashes of light, which was radiating from several TV screens inside the truck.

Suddenly the driver's side window slowly descended and a voice came from within. Had a bitch almost ready to hit the deck, thinking it was a roll-by or something. Can't just roll up on black folks all slow with dark ass tinted windows like that. I'm from Chi-town and I've seen it happen entirely too many times in the past. One minute a vehicle would creep by all slow and shit and the next thing you knew every- body would be running and ducking bullets. That shit is not cool!

My heart raced like crazy until I heard the driver's words, "Yo J.T., let's be out 'fore I haveta straighten one o' these niggas and make light shine through one o' they asses for not mindin' they fuckin' bizness out here."

When I was finally able to see who that voice belonged to I noticed that he was a light-brown skinned guy wearing a backwards fitted cap. He had an oversized platinum chain draped around his neck. When he stuck his hand out the window to thump ashes off the blunt he was smoking I saw that his wrist was wrapped in an ice-encrusted time- piece. I also noticed that his pinkie was laced in some nice sparkly shit as well.

Yep, street niggas, I thought while shifting my gaze from the driver back to J.T.

"Simmer down, nigga. I'm comin," J.T. replied to his boy just before the driver's side window went back up. He turned back to me. "I'm about to dip, but I wanna holla at you later. Like perhaps tomorrow…if you're not too busy. So, why don't you..." He paused to take out his iPhone, then said, "Your number would really make my night complete."

I thought for a brief moment, contemplating on whether or not to give him my number. After a few hesitant seconds I decided against it. I flipped my cell back open and replied, "Why don't I just get yours instead."

J.T. wasted no time in relaying his number to me as he watched me punch his digits into my phone and save the number.

After saying our goodbyes, with promises of hooking up in the near future, I watched as he strolled around and climbed into the passenger's side of the large truck.

I thought, *I gotta have me some of that! I hope his dick is as long as his dollars!*

While observing him walk away I noticed that he walked with a swagger that bordered the thin line between that of confidence and that of arrogance. Either way, that walk turned a sistahh on.

Minutes after J.T. had left, I was back inside Nine Three Five, retreiving my girl so we could be out because there was money to be made.

MIKE SANDERS

WAHIDA CLARK PRESENTS

ALONG CAME A SAVAGE

A NOVEL BY
JOE AWSUM
WITH WAHIDA CLARK

This is a work of fiction. Names, characters, places, and incidents either are the product of the author's imagination or are used fictitiously, and any resemblance to actual persons, living or dead, business establishments, events, or locales are entirely coincidental.

Wahida Clark Presents Publishing
60 Evergreen Place
Suite 904A
East Orange, New Jersey 07018
1(866)-910-6920
www.wclarkpublishing.com

Copyright 2014 © by Joe Awsum
All rights reserved. This book, or parts thereof, may not be reproduced in any form without permission.

Library of Congress Cataloging-In-Publication Data:
Joe Awsum
Along Came A Savage
ISBN 13-digit 978-1-944992-68-2 (Paper)
ISBN 13-digit 978-1-944992-89-7 (eBook)
ISBN 13-digit 978-1-947732-10-0 (Hardback)
LCCN: 2017914952
1. North Carolina- 3. Drug Trafficking- 4. African American- Fiction- 5. Urban Fiction- 6. Prison Life

Cover design and layout by Sebastien Stewart | seb@15-23.com
Interior design by NuanceArt@aCreativeNuance.com
Edited by Linda Wilson
Proofreader Rosalind Hamilton
Printed in USA

Chapter 1
Good Girl Gone Bad

Club Roxy was a hot new club on Chicago's South Side. Its elegance brought out all the ballers across the city, and tonight was no different. Bottles of Rosé Moët poured like bottled water after a track meet, as the males showed off their net worth by seeing who was going to buy the most bottles, especially since it was ladies' night.

Ladies' night always brought out all the bad bitches. They were coming out of the woodwork in every size and complexion. Most of them were dressed like the strippers who were going up and down the twenty stripper poles throughout the club.

"Bitch, I don't know how I let you drag me out tonight," a pretty, light-skinned female said to her brown-skinned friend.

"There you go, Tay Tay, you always tripping. Bitch, you can't tell me this spot ain't turnt up."

"I ain't gon' lie, Mesha, you always know where the turn up at."

"Bitch, that's what I do. Ain't shit changed since I moved away. I know it's been awhile since you been able to come out and play, so I wanted to make sure we did it right."

"You the one who disappeared."

"Hell, nah, bitch, you got with Mr. Ivy League Drug Lord and didn't even realize I was gone."

"First off, I was caught up in school, and Wayne is far from a drug lord."

"Bitch, please, he like the king of Chicago."
"Whatever!"

"School sure ain't paid for them diamonds on your wrist," Mesha said as she looked at the lights flickering off of Tay Tay's diamond ring and bracelet like a disco ball.

"Wayne ain't been in no streets; he been investing in real estate and business."

"Bitch, who you talking to? I been around you since we were little girls, and you know damn well, I *know* better." Tay Tay had almost forgotten that she was talking to her best friend and that Mesha knew her and Wayne's life like a book. She hadn't seen her in a year and a half, and Wayne had trained her to tell anyone that asked about his occupation that he was into real estate and owned businesses, even though he was the city's biggest cocaine and heroin supplier.

Tay Tay was about to reply as she attempted to gather her thoughts but was interrupted.

"Excuse me, ma, can a brother buy a fine lady like you a bottle?" a dark-skinned man with dreads said.

"I'll pass, I'm married," Tay Tay said before sipping from her glass of Hennessey.

"Damn, shorty, a nigga just trying to get to know you." "Damn, nigga, you can't hear or something? Shit, do it

look like we need a damn bottle? We good, nigga!" Mesha said before pouring the remainder of one of the three bottles of Moët they had on the table onto the floor, splashing on the dark-skinned man's shoes.

"First off, I ain't even talking to you. She a grown woman. She got a mouth of her own."

"Like I said, I'm married, now please move. You're blocking our view," Tay Tay said, knowing Mesha had no chill.

"Yeah, a'ight. I'll see you around."

"Doubt it. Now *poof*! be gone, nigga!" Mesha said before taking a swig from one of the two bottles of Moët she had left. The dark-skinned man just nodded his head slightly before walking away.

"Girl, you still crazy."

"Bitch, you know that sure ain't gon' change. But, anyways, when you get married? And even better, why the fuck wasn't I invited?"

"It ain't even like that. It was a spur-of-the-moment thing. I went on a trip to Vegas with Wayne, and the next thing you know, I was married," Tay Tay said, knowing she had taken off her ring to avoid this conversation tonight.

"Whatever, bitch. Anyways, let's toast to the bride then," Mesha said, holding up one of the remaining bottles of Moët for a toast. Tay Tay grabbed the other bottle and toasted with her best friend before gulping from it. Tay Tay was happy to be back around her girl. Lord knows she had so much going on in her life that she wanted to talk to Mesha about, but now wasn't the time. She hadn't had fun in a long time, and she wasn't about to waste a moment of it talking about her problems. Instead, she guzzled some more from her bottle.

***

The club didn't close until 5:00 a.m., but Tay Tay and Mesha left around two in the morning. They were drunk and starving as Tay Tay parked her white-on-white BMW 745 down the street from the hot dog stand so they could get some Jew Town polishes.

"Bitch, I'm about to buy everything on the menu," Tay said, passing Mesha the Backwoods full of loud they had been smoking on the ride there.

"Hell, yeah, you ain't never lied," Mesha said, giving her girl a high five.

Tay Tay and Mesha got out of the car trying to pull their tight miniskirts down over their curves. Both of them were thick like most of the video vixens you saw on TV. They only took a few steps when they heard a voice from behind them that made them stop and turn around.

"All I wanted was to get to know you. Then this bitch fronting me off in the club like I'm a sucka nigga or something," the dark-skinned man with the dreads from the club said.

"What the fuck! You some type of stalker or something?" Mesha asked.

"I'm sick of you bougie-ass bitches thinking you all that. I could buy both you hoes," the man said, throwing a handful of dollars at them like they were some strippers. Tay Tay was about to say something before Mesha's temper came out, but they were interrupted by a voice coming from behind them.

"Nigga, you got a problem with my wife? Hold my food, boo," a light brown-skinned man said, passing Tay Tay his food before kissing her on the cheek. Tay Tay had never met the man before, but something made her play along with him.

"It ain't even like that, fam."

"Well, it's like that now, nigga!" the man said before pulling his gun from his waistband and pressing the barrel of it against the man's forehead.

"Please! It's all a misunderstanding."

"You damn right, it's a misunderstanding. Now tell my wife and her friend, you sorry."

"I swear, I'm sorry."

"Y'all accept his apology?"

"Hell, nah, fuck him!" Mesha yelled out.

"Yeah, yeah, we forgive him," Tay Tay said, not wanting to get the man killed. She found herself turned on by this man defending her honor.

"Get the fuck out of here!" the brown-skinned man said, putting his gun back up. The dark-skinned man didn't say another word. He just turned and ran away.

"Well, I hate to get married and divorced on the same day, but I got an after-party to attend," he said. Tay Tay found herself hypnotized by his green eyes and muscular arms that were covered in tattoos.

"Bitch, say something," Mesha said, nudging her. "Yeah, my name is Tay Tay and this my girl, Mesha.

Thanks for helping us," Tay Tay said, snapping back to reality.

"It ain't nothing, sweetie. My name's Sa'vere. Look, since we're getting divorced, we might as well go out with a bang. Let me get y'all's food, and then I'll escort y'all to the celebrity after-party downtown. I heard Kanye and Drake supposed to fall through. So, what y'all say?"

"Bitch, he said Drake. Now you *know* he your favorite," Mesha said, excited.

Tay Tay hesitated for a second before speaking. "Fuck it, let's do it," she said. She had told Wayne she was staying in Chicago with her aunt for the weekend, especially since he wasn't fond of her hanging out with Mesha, or anyone else, for that matter. She knew it might be awhile before she saw Mesha again, so she planned on making the most it.

***

The line at the downtown hotel was almost wrapped around the building as Sa'vere, Tay Tay, and Mesha walked up.

"We ain't never gonna get in here. You know what, we appreciate you helping us tonight, but maybe this was a bad idea. Here, let me get you the money for the food," Tay Tay said, digging in her white Louis Vuitton purse.

"Chill, shorty, we good, trust me," Sa'vere said, pulling his phone out of his pocket and dialing a number. It rang for a few moments before someone answered on the other end.

"I'm outside," was all Sa'vere said before hanging up the phone.

"What's going on? I'm ready to get it poppin'," Mesha said.

"Well, y'all follow me then." Sa'vere walked them around to the dark alley behind the club. Tay Tay was ready to leave, but the back door of the building opened. Sa'vere shook the big security guard's hand before giving him a semihug like they'd known each other from way back.

"They with me."

"Well, you ladies better come on in," the security guard said, holding the door open for the women. The ladies followed closely behind Sa'vere as they walked through the kitchen while the kitchen workers continued working.

The third-floor penthouse suite was full of celebrities and the people who were lucky enough to get in.

"We 'bout to go to the ladies' room," Mesha said, grabbing Tay Tay by the arm.

"Okay, I'm about to get us some drinks," Sa'vere said, rubbing his 360 waves like he was brushing them as he looked Tay Tay in the eyes like no one else was in the room.

"Come on, girl, damn," Mesha said, pulling Tay Tay away. The line at the bathroom took almost twenty minutes to get inside. When Mesha's turn came up, she and Tay Tay went in together. Mesha turned the water on and went into her purse and pulled out a sandwich bag full of colorful Ecstasy pills. She quickly untied the bag, took out a pill, and popped it into her mouth before cuffing some water out of the running faucet in her hand and swallowing her pill.

"Damn, Mesha. What the fuck you on?" "Bitch, quit playing. Take a Wonder Man." "Girl, I don't know about that shit."

"Bitch, you said that the first time I gave you a blunt. Trust me . . . damn."

"Fuck it!" Tay Tay said, taking the pill from Mesha and swallowing it down. Mesha was two years older than Tay Tay and was always influencing her into doing stuff.

"Damn, bitch, you gotta live a little. This place is full of stars, and I'm about to catch me one."

"Whatever!" Tay Tay said, knowing her night was about to be next level fucking with Mesha.

The next couple of hours was full of liquor. Tay Tay didn't know if she was feeling the liquor or not, considering her pill had kicked in. She was having a ball, and before she knew it, she found herself just hanging with Sa'vere like she was his girl at the party as he was mingling with everyone.

"I need some air," Tay Tay said, feeling her body heating up from the Ecstasy.

"I got a suite here if you need to get away from all this craziness. These celebrities take partying to the next level."

"You know where Mesha's at?"

"After Kanye showed up, I ain't seen her since."

"Let me call her. I gotta make sure she straight. We came together, we leave together," Tay Tay said, pulling her phone out of her purse and pushing SEND on Mesha's number. The phone rang once before Mesha answered with loud music playing in the background that wasn't the same as Tay Tay's.

"Bitch, where the fuck you at?"

"Girl, I seen Yeezy. I'm on his heels."

"I'm about to go get some air. Call my phone if you need me."

"All right, girl, I gotta go. You interrupting my mission," Mesha said before hanging up.

"Well, I guess she's good. Let's go get some air."

The suite Sa'vere was in was pure luxury. She wouldn't have guessed that a street nigga like Sa'vere would be in a place like this. She wanted to ask him what he did for a living just out of curiosity, but she was a pretty good judge of character and could tell that he was a drug dealer.

"This place is nice."

"Thanks, this is some last-minute shit, but it'll do," Sa'vere said, laughing.

"It sure will do. This place gotta be $1,000 a night."

"It's $1,200, but I've seen better. This uppity shit ain't me. My peeps wanted me to come party, and that's what I did. Shit, you can give me a scale and a Motel 6 any day."

"I feel that shit." "You smoke?"

"Hell, yeah!" Tay Tay said, wanting to smoke some weed badly, hoping it would calm down her Ecstasy high.

"Good, let's smoke this uppity muthafucka out."

"Well, let's do it then," Tay Tay said, loving a real nigga that made his own rules.

For the next hour, Sa'vere rolled blunts of loud, and they smoked like they weren't in a high-class room. Tay Tay had been telling herself she was going to smoke a little more, and then leave. She knew she had no business alone with a man this fine and gutta like she liked. His conversation had her wrapped up; plus, it had been months since Wayne had been traveling the country on business and hadn't been around to talk about life or simply touch her. Tay Tay didn't know if it was the pill's side effect, but she found herself leaking in her panties just looking at Sa'vere.

"Damn, what time is it? I think I need to be finding Mesha," Tay Tay said as they finished the second blunt.

"It's 4:30."

"Damn, it's late."

"I understand. Well, it has been nice being married to you for a day."

"It's been nice being married to you as well," Tay Tay said, giving Sa'vere a hug as they approached the door. The hug was meant to be short, but Tay Tay found herself holding onto his muscular structure. *Bitch, get out the door,* she thought, but her body was saying, "take me now." Sa'vere pulled away just enough to look deep into Tay Tay's eyes like he was reading her soul. Tay Tay hesitated at first, but before she knew it, her lips were pressed against his. Their passion was like an explosion, their tongues meeting, the fuse that ignited it. Sa'vere picked her up off her feet, and her thick thighs wrapped around him instantly as they continued to kiss. She didn't know where Sa'vere was taking her, but she was ready to go.

Within minutes, she found herself on the granite countertop in the kitchen.

"Oh shit, what am I doing?" Tay Tay whispered out loud as Sa'vere began sucking on her neck aggressively before pulling her perfect titties out of her tight shirt. He took those titties and pushed them together before sucking hard on both erect nipples, back and forth, until

Tay Tay was moaning slightly. The way he moved his tongue, she couldn't do anything but wonder how it would feel on her dripping-wet pussy. She didn't have to wait long to find out as Sa'vere pulled her white lace panties to the side and dove face-first into her ocean of pleasure.

"Oh my God!" Tay Tay yelled out as Sa'vere's tongue flicked across her swollen clit.

"God ain't gonna save you. Bitch, feed me that pussy!" Sa'vere said before diving back into her sweetness. Sa'vere's words made Tay Tay want to come everywhere. Before she knew it, she was holding both cabinet handles with her feet flat on the countertop as she fucked his face.

Sa'vere accepted the challenge as Tay Tay continued grinding her pussy in the air and all across his tongue. His arms cuffed her thighs and lifted her off the counter, all the while still eating her pussy as she held onto the cabinet handles.

"Oh shit, you gonna make me come everywhere!" Tay Tay screamed out as her body began convulsing, come leaking out of her pussy and into his mouth. Sa'vere didn't give her a chance to recover. He just picked her up and threw her across his shoulder like a caveman. Tay Tay had never been manhandled like this before and every second of it had her wanting to be fucked even more. Sa'vere threw her on the huge bed, and he watched her like a wild animal eyeing at his prey. Tay Tay bit her bottom lip as he took his shirt off before pulling his rock-hard dick out of his pants. He rolled a condom on, and before Tay Tay could blink, he had snatched her to the end of the bed and plunged his big dick deep inside her tight, wet pussy. The pleasure outweighed the pain, and Tay Tay couldn't do anything but grab the sheets for the ride.

"Damn, you feel like you in my stomach."

"I'm about to get all in this phat-ass pussy," Sa'vere said, grabbing her by both her ankles, spreading her thick thighs all the way apart as he stirred in that pussy like some macaroni. His stroke was slow at first, but his aggression took over after about a minute, and Tay Tay found herself getting fucked like never before.

"Oh shit, nigga, you killing this pussy!" Tay Tay screamed out as she began coming again . . . and again as he continued to beat that pussy like it stole something. Sa'vere pulled his dick out and flipped her over before digging inside her dripping-wet pussy from the back. He showed her no mercy as he pounded her from the back. Tay Tay had to bite the bedsheets to stop from screaming his name to the heavens above.

Tay Tay was happy when Sa'vere reached his climax, and she couldn't do anything but lay across the bed. She looked back at him, and he was standing there like a savage. That was the last thing she remembered before passing out.

***

Tay Tay woke up around 7:00 a.m. The effects of the Ecstasy wouldn't allow her to stay asleep, but the ringing of her phone was what woke her up. She was half-dressed as she looked around for Sa'vere, but she didn't see him. Then she heard the shower running and saw the bathroom door was cracked. She hopped out of the bed and went to the bathroom door and peeped inside. She could see Sa'vere's silhouette through the steamy glass shower doors. She quickly ran and got her phone out of her purse and went into the kitchen. She calmed herself down before dialing the number back that had already called four times.

"Good morning." "Morning, Wayne."

"I called you a bunch of times. Is there something wrong with your phone?"

"I was asleep."

"I told you no matter what time I call, you gotta answer this phone, Taylor. This ain't no game. Anything could be happening, and your fucking excuse is you were fucking sleeping. This is unacceptable!"

"I know, Wayne. I was up late taking care of my aunt." "Well, get yourself together and get home. I need you to

do something for me." "Okay."

"I hope your aunt gets better," he said before hanging up in her face. Tay Tay hated Wayne's voice at that moment. She knew he didn't care about her aunt and was just saying that to be funny. She put her phone on the counter and walked back toward the room. By the time she got to the bedroom, she was butt naked and headed straight for the bathroom. It was steamy from the hot water as she entered the room. She walked like a woman with purpose as she opened the shower door.

"Let me help you with that," she said, watching the water drip off his dick. He became hard instantly looking at her sexy body. Tay Tay didn't give him time to react. She knew what she wanted, and she was going to get it. She grabbed his swollen dick and stroked it before squatting down eye-to-eye with the dick. Sa'vere looked down at her as she took him in her mouth slowly, then slurped on it like she would a Popsicle in the summertime. Tay Tay looked up into his eyes as she continued to jerk his rock-hard dick off on her thick, wet lips.

"Bitch, quit playing and suck this dick," Sa'vere said, grabbing the back of her head and pushing his dick back in her mouth. She moaned slightly, loving his aggressive nature as his dick pounded against the back of her throat.

"Damn, girl, I'll fuck you all in your mouth," Sa'vere said, grabbing her head with both hands. Tay Tay wanted that dick all down her throat, and Sa'vere was giving her what she desired, and more. Tay Tay could taste come leaking into her mouth, so she pulled his dick out and continued stroking it as she put his balls gently in her mouth.

"Shit, bitch!" Sa'vere said, loving the freak in Tay Tay. Tay Tay took his balls out of her mouth, then began licking her tongue up from the bottom of his shaft until she reached the head, making come squirt out in her face and mouth like a volcano had erupted.

"Shit!" Sa'vere moaned, putting his hand against the wall for balance as she sucked the head of his dick making sure she got every last drop.

"Now, we officially divorced," Tay Tay said, standing up and walking out of the shower.

Sa'vere couldn't do nothing but shake his head looking at all that ass walking out of his shower. He was going to let her walk away but couldn't. Tay Tay had just got out of the bathroom when she heard the sound of Sa'vere walking fast behind her. She turned around just as he got to her. Suddenly, she was up in his arms with her legs wrapped around his waist. He took both of them straight to the bed. His dick slid right into her wet, throbbing pussy. He grinded all in that pussy until her nails were lodged in his back.

"Oh, Sa'vere, you keep hitting my spot, daddy!"

Sa'vere could feel her pussy pulsating around his dick, so he began speeding up until you could hear Tay

Tay's pussy leaking. Her thighs trembled hard around his body, and her nails in his flesh made her look like she was holding on for dear life.

"Right there, right there. Oh shit, I ain't never felt like this. I'm about to come all over that big-ass dick." No sooner than the words left her lips, she had come running all over his dick. Sa'vere really began beating that pussy hard and fast, making Tay Tay scream out and begin shaking again.

"Oh shit, nigga, I'm coming again!" Sa'vere could feel her wetness increase and had no choice but to pull his dick out and come all over Tay Tay's pussy. "Now we're divorced, bitch."

"Whatever, nigga," Tay Tay said, lying there as her body continued to tremble in pleasure. Sa'vere found himself shaking his head again, knowing he had broken his number one and number two rule, but he liked it.

***

"Well, you be safe. If you ever change your mind about divorcing me, here's my number." Tay Tay looked at the piece of paper Sa'vere was holding as he leaned in her window.

"I guess. Bye," she replied, taking the number like she didn't want it before letting the window up on him. He could see her smiling through her tinted window as she backed up. Sa'vere just stood there with a devilish grin on his face, watching her pull off. As soon as her BMW disappeared in traffic, a voice from behind got Sa'vere's attention.

"Damn, nigga, what the fuck is you doing? We got shit to do."

"I'm coming, Trell. Shit. Quit sweating me, nigga," Sa'vere said, talking to the dark-skinned man with the dreads that he had pulled the gun on last night for Tay Tay and Mesha.

"Nigga, you over here all glossy-eyed and shit, watching the bitch leave. Nigga, don't fuck this money up."

"Nigga, get your ugly ass in the car. I know what the fuck I'm doing. When have I ever missed my target?" Sa'vere asked, pausing, waiting on Trell to answer.

"Exactly. Now get your ass in the damn car."

"Nigga, fuck you!" Trell said, getting in the car with his best friend. He knew Sa'vere was a ladies' man and made both of them a good living doing it.

"That bitch just like the rest, nigga; this money in the bank," Sa'vere said with his million-dollar smile. Being a professional side nigga wasn't his career of choice. It was a career that chose him. He knew there was a lot of money on the line with Tay Tay. He had already violated two of his own personal rules of his hustle which was never have sex but one time on the first night, and never ever have unprotected sex. Both of those built too many emotions and, in this game, there was no room for feelings or fuckups, especially at this level. Last time he had fucked up, it got him stuck in this career. Sa'vere knew Tay Tay was on his mind, and he couldn't deny it. He was going to have to shake the shit off because shit was about to get real. Lighting a cigarette, he blew the smoke out the window as he and Trell made their way through traffic.

Copyright © 1987 by Al Dickens. All rights reserved.

The responsibility for the Theology expressed in this book is entirely that of the author, Al Dickens.

"Literature should not be suppressed merely because it offends the moral code of the censor."
-*Supreme Court Justice*
  William O.
  Douglass
Dissent, Roth vs. U.S. 354 & U.S. 476-(1957)

Published by:
Yah Yah Publications
60 Evergreen Place Suite
904 East Orange, NJ 07018
www.yahyahpublications.com

An imprint of:
Wahida Clark Presents Publishing
60 Evergreen Place
Suite 904 East Orange, NJ
07018
973-678-9982 • www.wclarkpublishing.com

ISBN 13 DIGIT 978-0-9759646-8-2
ISBN 10 DIGIT 0-9759646-7-4

Library of Congress Control Number: 2004351502 Urban, Philosophy, Self-Help, Fiction, African American, Motivation, Fables, Spiritual.

Book layout design by: Nuance_Art.*. nuanceart@gmail.com
Cover design by: Baja Wakiri Ukweli
1st Printing 1973 5 4 3 2 1

Chapter One

DOTTIE

My name is Rudy Hawkins, and I'm a reporter for the Essex Weekly News, one of the few black owned and black operated newspapers in the city of Newark, New Jersey. Dottie (Dorothy Schleifa), a beautiful black sister and typist in the office, was the first to inform me of the man called Uncle Yah Yah.

It was Monday morning and the office was alive with the usual clang bang, hustle, and bustle noises of a press room. I was sitting at my desk putting the finishing touches on an article dealing with police corruption, when I noticed it was almost time for the 10:00 a.m. coffee break. Just then Bill Diamonds, one of our best reporters, rushed into the office shouting:

"I got it, I got it!"

Some of the reporters gathered around him to hear the news.

"I've got an exclusive on that sixteen-year-old kid who raped those nine old ladies."

Bill had every right to be excited. He had been following that case for weeks. He threw his hands in the air in a gesture of victory and strutted with his chest out like a peacock. He spoke to the crowd in rapid fire of the details in the young man's confession.

"His aunt was his first victim, but she never reported it, and there are two others that he confessed to raping who also didn't report it," Bill explained.

"Why did he only rape women in their 50's and 60's?" Someone in the crowd wanted to know.

"He told me that he was seduced by an old woman when he was fourteen, which was his first sexual experience, and since then he has only desired older women," Bill answered.

All this sex talk made me remember Dottie. It was time for me to renew my attempt at seducing her. I found Dottie at her desk sipping coffee and looking rather sober. So I decided to make some outlandish advances to humor her.

"What's happening Cup Cake? I've got a quarter. Heads you kiss me, tails I kiss you. What have you got, heads or tails?" I asked as I showed her the quarter in the palm of my hand.

"No thank you Rudy," was her curt reply.

"No thank you?" I asked as I repeated her words in a show of great disappointment. "Well that's too bad for you Dottie. I was going to give you my Monday morning special, but you blew it."

"Why don't you give your wife the Monday morning special?"

"My wife doesn't know how to act when I give her the Monday morning special. She gets pregnant and stuff like that."

Dottie had to laugh in spite of herself. The ice was now broken and she began to tell me about her vacation. I had tried for one whole year to get Dottie to go on a date with me, but the closest I could get to her was the 10:00 a.m. coffee break. Usually, she didn't talk much, but now, her first day back in the office, I was beginning to think she would never stop talking.

Dottie had spent a week at Paradise Gardens—a black resort—where she met a wise old man. Paradise Gardens is located in upstate New York, in a little place called Cuddibackville. The hills, the mountains, the forests, the rushing streams, and lakes filled with leaping trout, are pretty much the same today, in Cuddibackville as they were 100 years ago. Small wonder that it's a paradise for vacationers.

For ten minutes I listened to Dottie describing the joy she found in Paradise Gardens, but the acme of her pleasure, she said, was when she met an old man called Uncle Yah Yah. She just couldn't tell me enough about this old guy.

"Uncle Yah Yah, is not the Holy preacher type person most people think him to be. He's just like you and me, and he doesn't preach all that spooky stuff about sinners burning in hell after they die. There's nothing after death. If we don't get any heaven now, while we live, we just don't get any. God created heaven and hell. Both complement each other. The angels are sent from heaven into hell and the sinner is sent from hell to heaven and when everyone understands that law, there will be no more good and evil and we'll have some peace for a change. You should hear some of the stories he told Rudy. They all have a parable and he uses animals as his characters. I'm sure you would've enjoyed listening to his stories. I felt so good sitting there listening to Uncle Yah Yah, I didn't want to leave."

I had to interrupt her. Dottie was beginning to bore me, plus I was jealous because I could see that she was really impressed with this old man.

"Hey Dottie, what are you doing, writing a book on the guy or something?"

She gave me a hard look. No, it was more like a cold stare. I was beginning to feel sorry for my show of sarcasm. Just then her face lit up like a Christmas tree.

"Rudy! That's it. You're a genius. Why didn't I think of that? You've got to do it Rudy, please!"

"Dottie, wait a minute. I know that I'm a genius and all that, but will you please tell me what the hell you're talking about?"

"You said it Rudy. You said write a book on Uncle Yah Yah. Will you do it, please, for me? All you have to do is go to Paradise Gardens and interview him. Will you do it?"

At this point I had to slow down and take a better look at what was happening. This was the first time Dottie ever asked me for a favor — just the chance I've been waiting for. If I played my hand right I'd have Dottie exactly where I wanted her.

"You really want me to do a story on this guy, don't you?"

"Yes, I really do."

"Well I'll tell you what I'm going to do. I'll check it out with the boss and if it's O.K., then I'll do it on one condition."

"What are you up to?" she asked with a look of contempt.

"Don't get scared. I just want you to promise me a date if I get the story published. Now is that asking too much?"

"A date?" she asked indignantly.

"Come on Dottie, be reasonable. You spend hours every day trying to make yourself attractive and desirable. You wouldn't even leave the house if you weren't sure you were looking just right. Being a professional girl watcher, that I am, naturally I am attracted to you. I really appreciate all that you've done to make yourself beautiful and I tell you as much. Instead of you being flattered and saying it's good of me to notice, you are trying to condemn me. Where is the justice in that? Would you prefer a dude too dumb to notice or value your beauty? Who would look upon you as commonplace? Let's face it Dottie. You and I can see eye to eye. Think about it. All I'm asking you for girl is just one little ole date."

She thought about it for a few seconds and then said, "It's a deal. But not because of any of that garbage you're trying to feed me. It's because of Uncle Yah Yah."

Coffee break was over, Dottie went back to her desk and I went to see the boss.

WAHIDA CLARK PRESENTS

URBAN ISIS PART 1: REVOLUTION

A NOVEL BY
WILLIE GROSS JR.
WITH WAHIDA CLARK

This is a work of fiction. Names, characters, places, and incidents either are the product of the author's imagination or are used fictitiously, and any resemblance to actual persons, living or dead, business establishments, events, or locales are entirely coincidental.

Wahida Clark Presents Publishing
60 Evergreen Place
Suite 904A
East Orange, New Jersey 07018
1(866)-910-6920
www.wclarkpublishing.com

Copyright 2019 © by Willie Gross Jr

All rights reserved. This book, or parts thereof, may not be reproduced in any form without permission.

Library of Congress Cataloging-In-Publication Data:
Willie Gross Jr with Wahida Clark
Urban Isis Part 1
ISBN 13-digit 9781947732377 (paper)
ISBN 13-digit 9781947732421 (ebook)

LCCN: 2017904240

1. Sex - 2. Lies - 3. social - 4. African American- –
5. futuristic - 6. Violence - 7. Relationships

Cover design and layout by Nuance Art, LLC
Book design by www.artdiggs.com
Edited by Linda Wilson
Proof-reader Rosalind Hamilton
Printed in USA

Introduction

Let us, reader and writer, agree on only what's real, numbers, and reality, primarily because they don't lie! Tragically, the drug usage among our teenagers of today has steadily increased year after year after year. The problem with this reality is it infringes upon the productivity of our expected torchbearers of tomorrow—the dreamers, the inventors, the pioneers of new technologies that'll spearhead breakthroughs in scientific research, futuristically enabling this nation to remain ahead of and relevant to every other nation.

Yet, as a nation, it seems as though we won't decide which of the two is more important: the drugs or the torchbearers. It is one thing to say we are who we say we are as a nation; yet, we steadily and with regularity, do the opposite. So, we ask ourselves, those confused and concerned by these truths . . . *What's the plan?* Or, *who's doing the planning?*

Yes, politics, greed, economics, fear, arrogance, and hate . . . All recipes for the gradual destruction of a nation and its torchbearers! These are critical components designed to suppress the brilliance, idealism, and productivity of our young, bright minds. The critical thinkers in possession of solutions to common problems plaguing our society, our neighbourhoods, our schools, and ultimately . . . our generations!

But, today, we're thinking critically! We'll start designing what our minds, hearts, and souls are in total agreement with. It's the right thing to do. We won't fool ourselves into selfish decision making cantered around who's right. We're thinking long-range, making decisions for the whole, predicated on solid advice in doing what's right!

Yes, it's fiction—only because we're living in a society controlled by a few—and their only concern is always *their* needs. So, to do what's right in this society would be to them, fictitious. Now, we've established that their fiction is really a reality in the real world, so let's talk building! No hidden agendas . . . hands on the table . . . real-life, drama-type of building.

Let's dream again; let's rewind our memories; let's go back to when all of us knew as pre-schoolers and young grade-schoolers what we wanted to be in life. Let's heal instead of kill the dreams of tomorrow. Feel me? Let's build this dynasty alongside James Johnson. Let's come together in our minds, then think critically about our tomorrows . . . our hopes, our struggles, our accomplishments, our defeats, our victories, and, yes, even our demise. But more importantly, let's leave something good behind. Let's do *that*!

Let's resolve to understand why we struggle, get it all out of our system, then never look back, because the struggle isn't our identity. It was only made to look that way. That's why we accepted it!

In essence, we tear down the fake, then replace it with the real. Let's not automatically think defeat when we go up against the powers that be! Remember, *they're* the reason why we're in this mess! Look, we're building in this book, the right way too, reality!

Let's realize our propensity to be a great people first; *then* we can talk that great nation stuff. Keep turning pages; you'll see, we're people building. This way, we can't lose because we must be a great people before we can be a great nation. You agree? But it's not going to be pretty. Old habits die hard! But they *do* die, and that's James Johnson's only concern!

Now, let all of us envision ourselves in powerful positions, just like the powerful people of today, then ponder . . . If I ruled the world, what would I do? Who would I be? What, then, would be *my* contribution to society? Imagine *that*!

Let's face reality . . . No matter how much good we do in life, it'll never be enough to satisfy the haters. It's what they do best. So keep turning pages to see how James dealt with those haters. How he masterfully played a game they invented.

Let's look at the big picture—the future! Let's all agree . . . Tomorrow is for those who prepare for it today. Let's begin with the real . . . "Urban Isis, Part 1: The Revolution"!

CHAPTER 1
The Blueprint

The dark, chilly night and semi-deserted parking lot provided a perfect canopy for mischief. The clean-shaven Caucasian male acknowledged this as he walked with deliberate haste en route to his vehicle. He looked every bit the part of an ivy leaguer: starch white shirt, blue tie, and blue duck head slacks. His expensive leather briefcase swung in time with his steps. A quick glance toward the small end of the parking lot revealed an open Krispy Kreme doughnut shop. The wonderful smell of deep-fried sweet dough floated in the air like clouds.

As he approached his vehicle, an Arab dressed in traditional Muslim attire, slipped behind him and wrapped his right arm around his victim's damp neck and placed his left arm behind his head and squeezed.

The Ivy-leaguer put up a struggle, kicking and twisting but his body went limp, and the offender relieved him of his briefcase.

The attack reminded the carefully observant James of poetry— a concentrated imaginative awareness of experience, chosen and arranged to create a specific emotional response. James too had been stalking the victim for the past two days, but for different reasons, it seemed. The briefcase was supposed to have contained a large amount of money. The information he possessed came from an employee at the tech company who was dying for his attention. She estimated it to be well over $200,000. They agreed on a ten percent split, provided the information checked out. So, here he was parked for a second night ducked down in a stolen black Regal. Wearing all black, and his favorite black New Orleans Saints cap pulled down snug on his head.

With plans of only retrieving the briefcase, and by any means necessary, if it came down to that, James followed the van. It was now 11:35 p.m. on a Friday night. The Arab's final destination was a warehouse in New Orleans east. Hastily, James exited the Regal and crossed the dark, deserted parking lot with his Glock 40 planted against his leg.

At first James leaned up against the building, but now circled it in search of an entrance. He found none. On his second search, he located an air conditioning ventilation grill. It was approximately four feet by four feet. *Perfect*. He immediately began kicking it in until he was able to peel enough of an entrance to climb through.

The hole was behind a crowded room of big barrels of liquid he held no concern for, as he slowly crept about the room blindly. He could now see a lit entrance. The smelly fumes made James assume that oil was inside the barrels.

From the shadows, James peeped out into the hallway and into the warehouse strategically arranged like an air traffic control tower on one side, and a torture chamber on the other. The kidnapped victim was seated in an iron chair fitted with iron bracelets that secured his hands and legs to the chair. The kidnapper was seated directly in front of the victim.

"What business did you have in my country other than as a missionary worker?" the Arab asked evenly.

"None, sir. Please," the Caucasian male nervously answered while sweat leaked down his face. "Please . . . I swear. I was just trying to help your people."

"I'll ask this another way. What business did you have in my country other than missionary work?" The kidnapper never raised his voice, exhibiting the utmost control as an interrogator.

After subtly leaving his chair, the Arab returned with a long sparkling sword. He placed it on a table nearby that also held the briefcase James had come for.

Ivy Leaguer danced in his seat, then cried out, "Okay, okay. I'll tell you . . . I provided a . . . a location," the victim frantically spoke with nervous candor in an attempt to right his perceived wrong. "I'm sorry. I had to . . . They-they made me . . . Oh my *God* I'm so sorry! Please, please don't!" he begged.

Slowly, the Arab walked over to the wall, then flipped a switch. From the ceiling, a thick braided rope with a noose at the end mechanically descended. The victim pleaded, wiggled, and cried out, but to no avail—the noose was now fitted around his neck.

James watched in amazement as the Middle Easterner held up the sword, then chopped off both arms of the victim to the elbows, then his legs to the knees. The victim screamed in agony as blood splashed, skeeted, and oozed out of the wounds. But before he could faint, another switch was flipped, and the victim was sprung into the air by the rope, breaking his neck instantly. The body twisted violently in the air, causing it to rain blood.

The man with the long gray and white beard placed the sword on the table and was now accessing his computer system. James looked from the Arab to the briefcase, trying to determine how he could get what he wanted, then live to enjoy it. After determining

(1) they were alone, and (2) he had the ups and planned on keeping it; he slowly eased out into the opening with the gun in his right hand, still lying comfortably against his leg.

Sensing his presence, the man calmly scratched his head through his black turban. He turned in the chair, and then stood to fearlessly face James. James stared back at the man, but couldn't get a read on him.

"As salaam Alaikum," James offered as his greeting. "Wa alaikum as salaam," the Arab responded.

They both seemed to relax.

"May I help you?" the man questioned, in the most respectful of manners.

"I've been staking out your victim for a couple of days in regard to that briefcase over there." James nodded.

"Do you know of its contents?" the man asked.

"I know what's *supposed* to be there. My inside connect has never been wrong."

"And if what you seek isn't there?"

"Then I've been misled."

"I've been surveilling this person for two months. So, how do we determine *who* has the rights to the briefcase?"

James tapped the gun against his leg. Closely taking in the man's visage from head to foot, he'd made out the Arab's true identity. He now possessed the ups and the deal-breaker. "Aren't you aware of the $25 million bounty on your head? Dead or alive. Osama bin Laden."

Osama smiled and shifted his gaze toward the gun being patted against the young black man's leg. "I'm very aware of it," he confessed.

"So, can I have my briefcase now?" James tilted his head slightly.

"And that's it?" The man shrugged lightly. "That's the only thing I came for."

Wrinkles appeared in Osama's forehead. James knew Osama was both intrigued and puzzled. Now he wondered if the man was bold enough to express the better move.

"So, what's his transgression?" James focused on the guy still twisting slowly in the air.

"He's a double-agent. By day he was on our front lines appearing to be a missionary to our people, and by night he's feeding the United States coordinates to launch their drone attacks."

"What will you do with his body?" "You really must know?" Osama asked. "Flatter me," James stated.

"Dispose of it after I take pictures to post as a warning to other spies." He paused briefly before speaking. "You do know our countries are at war because of your country's occupation of my country?"

"Don't follow politics. I focus on my survival," James stated firmly.

"And what exactly is your true goal in life besides survival, which is a basic animal instinct?" He placed his thumb and forefinger on his bearded chin.

"To be in a position to one day make a difference." *Where is this conversation going?* James wondered, but nevertheless, he kept his eyes on the briefcase the entire time.

"Then that is your purpose. Now, how do you intend on reaching this feat?"

"I need . . . a break in life. Just one . . ." he emphasized, pointing the gun toward the briefcase.

"No," Osama reasoned. "You need structure, strategy, and faith. With those qualities present, it gives you the best chance to succeed." Osama grabbed his blood-stained sword to pick up the briefcase by its handle. It slid down on the sword's sharp incline toward Osama's clasped hands on the grip. He left the briefcase there, dangling against the guard, just like the body above their heads.

"I have none of those qualities, and heart isn't on that list, so that makes me doomed, right?" Instantly, James stepped forward and got a good grip on the briefcase's handle. The two men locked gazes.

"If what you say you have is true, then the qualities I spoke of are already present, and you need only to hone your skills." With one forceful jerk of his sword, Osama broke the intruder's grasp on the briefcase.

"And how does all this *honing* occur while I'm struggling to take care of my family, stay out of the penitentiary, and stay alive?" James asked, with a face void of emotion. He was getting pissed with the line of questioning and the fact that $200,000 had just been knocked away from his fingertips.

"Where are your parents, if I may ask?"

"I'd rather not speak of my parents," James stated in an almost threatening tone with a hardened glare.

"Any other family?" Osama asked, now pointing the sword at James' chest.

"Kinda sorta," James said with reluctance, careful not to divulge too much info. Not knowing how the present situation would play out, he raised the gun at a thirty-degree angle, prepared to deliver a shot to Osama's heart.

"Do you know what a network consists of?" Osama looked down at the gun briefly, unfazed.

"I hate guessing, so why don't you explain."

"I'd rather you tell me what you think it is," he insisted, lowering the sword so the briefcase slid toward James.

James let his right hand holding the gun, rest at his side. He released a small sigh. "In street terminology, I'd say it's a group of people working to achieve the same goals."

Osama half turned and set the briefcase and sword back on the table and began clapping. "Your definition was better than mine, and I'm prepared to offer you access to this network, as well as the briefcase you desire. Being it is reasonably clear that you're a man of principle, and we also have a common foe."

"And who would that be?" James narrowed his brows in genuine curiosity.

"The ones in control—the powers that be."

"And how did you come to that conclusion?" James asked. "Simple. You never seriously considered collecting the bounty on my head, even though the opportunity presented itself." "And?"

"And it's clear you oppose killing without a reason, or for the powers that be. You've acknowledged our plights are different, yet we're fighting the same system."

"How could you know about my plight?" James' nostrils flared. "Because I knew of your people's struggle throughout history.

You are no different than the last generation of young black males still experiencing racial bigotry even as adults."

Instinctively, James stole a quick glance at the hangman. "That should never be you," Osama stated, after observing James' brief gaze at the victim. "Why's that?"

"Because you possess loyalty to your cause and to those cut from the same cloth. But you must remember, every man confessing loyalty isn't who he says he is. I can teach you to spot them, test them, and destroy them." He picked up the briefcase and held it toward James.

"Then *that* sounds like a winner," James stated, placing the Glock 40 in his waistband. He gripped his $200,000 bounty, then walked over to embrace Osama. "You must really love your countrymen, braving your chances here in America." he asked, breaking their contact.

"It is because of that love that I took the chance of coming here." Osama folded his arms across his chest.

James thought about Osama's answer, then focused on the body still suspended in mid-air. *Damn, I hope this isn't a trap*, he thought. "My mother was that type of person to the community. She instilled in us the love of our neighbor and country. But she could not be to her country what she was to her community. She was just a hardworking, loving pillar in the community. I want to succeed where she could not."

"You must become just as big as your country in order to succeed on that level, my friend."

"Is that a realistic goal?" James smirked.

"When you think of my country—who do you think of?" "That's easy! Osama bin Laden," James stated.

"So, it is possible—no matter in what way you're thought of." "Yet, being America's Most Wanted isn't the recipe for the

changes I'd like to make."

"Then you must become America's most loved," Osama insisted.

"And how would I succeed at that?"

"You begin with the deadly venom in order to get the antidote. That my friend, will be your task, and my duty is to help you realize this goal is realistically possible."

"The world all of a sudden has gotten much larger," James stated, taking a few steps back to begin making his exit. He wasn't crazy enough to turn his back on Osama.

"Then your vision must do the same. Remember, a true visionary gives us a glimpse of the future in his work today," Osama assured him. "We will meet again."

James never envisioned abandoning his mother's vision of what a community should be. But what could he do to affect not only his community, but every community in the country? In order to determine the solution to the problem, he'd have to definitely identify the cause. He knew in most communities he would try to help, that cause would be drugs. And many days he'd sold these same drugs in order to feed his family—a real life catch-22. Yet the real trick would be to win with drugs and build stronger communities all over the world in light of this union.

Printed by Libri Plureos GmbH in Hamburg, Germany